THE WHISPERING STATUE

Nancy Drew is asked to solve a puzzling mystery and immediately is confronted with another, even more complicated. The first one concerns a valuable collection of rare books that Mrs. Horace Merriam commissioned a supposedly reputable art dealer to sell, but she now suspects that the man is a swindler. The second mystery revolves around the baffling theft of a beautiful marble statue.

To solve both mysteries, the famous young detective disguises herself and assumes a false identity. Despite these precautions, danger stalks Nancy's every move. An attempted kidnapping, a nearly disastrous sailboat collision, and an encounter with a dishonest sculptor are just a few of the exciting challenges that Nancy is faced with as she gathers evidence against a clever ring of art thieves.

You will enjoy every moment of this thrill-packed story of how Nancy and her friends combine detective work and summer fun at a seaside resort.

Could she depend on her disguise not to be recognized?
Nancy wondered

NANCY DREW MYSTERY STORIES

The Whispering Statue

BY CAROLYN KEENE

GROSSET & DUNLAP

Publishers • New York

Contents

The Whispering
Statue

CHAPTER I

Three-Way Alarm

"Nancy, you're kidding. No statue can whisper!"

A twinkle came into Nancy Drew's blue eyes. She tossed back her reddish-gold hair and looked at the slender, athletic girl standing in front of her. "George, the statue I'm talking about used to whisper before it disappeared."

A third girl in the Drews' attractive living room, Bess Marvin, spoke up. "Where is this marvel?" She was blond and slightly plump and dark-haired George Fayne's cousin.

George grinned. "The marvelous marble!" The other two girls laughed.

Nancy said, "I don't know anything more about it, but Dad has a client coming to dinner who will explain everything. She has a case for him and he hinted that he wants you girls and me to help solve a mystery in connection with it."

"Sounds great!" George remarked.

Bess, more cautious than her cousin, looked at Nancy. "Will it be a nice straight mystery, or one that's going to scare the wits out of me?" Nancy said she knew nothing about the case.

Just then Mr. Drew's car pulled into the circular driveway of his brick Colonial home, which stood well back from the street. The front lawn was wide with attractive shrubs and flowers. He helped a woman of about forty from the car and escorted her to the front entrance. She was tall, slender, and pretty. Nancy hurried to open the door.

"Hello, dear," her father said. "Nancy, this is Mrs. Merriam."

Nancy shook hands and she and Mrs. Merriam exchanged smiles.

"I feel so relieved to be here," the caller said. "Unwittingly I seem to have become involved in a mystery with a legal angle to it. Your father was recommended to me as a leading attorney."

"And he is too," Nancy hastened to say. She took Mrs. Merriam's summer coat and gloves, and the three walked into the living room.

"Mrs. Merriam, I'd like you to meet my friends Bess Marvin and George Fayne," Nancy said. Smiling, she added, "They're part of my detective force, so you may speak freely in front of them."

Mrs. Merriam proved to be a charming person. She was introduced to Mrs. Hannah Gruen, who had been the Drews' housekeeper since Nancy was three years old. Upon the death of the little girl's mother, Hannah had assumed the responsibility of helping to rear Nancy. Mrs. Gruen was a level-headed and kindly person who always worried about Nancy while she was solving a mystery.

"Dinner is served," she announced. "Is everyone ready to go to the table?"

Mr. Drew laughed. "Ready and starving. I hope you have some of my favorites tonight."

While the Drew family and their guests ate, the lawyer suggested that his new client tell her story.

"I live in Waterford on the coast," she said. "Some time ago an uncle of mine left me a very fine library of books. Hundreds of them. My home is too small to accommodate them all, so my husband urged me to sell the collection.

"Horace is away frequently on business and left all the negotiations to me. I went to Willis Basswood in town—he runs a high-class art gallery and bookshop—to see if he could sell the volumes for me."

Mrs. Merriam went on to say that Mr. Basswood had agreed, and would take twenty-five percent of each sale as his fee.

"At first everything seemed to go well. Mr. Basswood was able to get a high price for certain volumes, not so much for others. He gave me receipts for everything. Then suddenly the money stopped coming. When I asked him why, he said that the books were not selling."

As she paused, Mr. Drew remarked, "Now Mrs. Merriam has become suspicious of the man and feels that perhaps he's disposing of them but not giving her the money."

Before the lawyer could explain further, he and the others at the dinner table were startled by the ringing of the front and back doorbells and the telephone.

"Excuse me," said Mr. Drew and went toward the front door.

Hannah made her way to the back door, while Nancy answered the wall telephone in the kitchen. A harsh voice on the other end of the line asked, "Drew residence?"

"Yes. Whom do you want?" Nancy queried.

The caller rasped, "You tell Mrs. Merriam to shut up or she'll get hurt and you people too!" The caller slammed down the instrument.

By this time Hannah had opened the back door. To her amazement a burly masked man stepped inside and knocked her to the floor. Simultaneously there was a yell from the front hall. Bess and George appeared and went to aid Hannah, while Nancy rushed out of the kitchen to help her father. George leaped forward and with a neat judo hold tossed Hannah's assailant over on his back.

Hannah jumped up and together she and the girls grabbed the intruder. But he fought fiercely

"Tell Mrs. Merriam to shut up or you people will get hurt!" the telephone caller rasped

and with a sharp twist pulled free and ran out the open door.

Meanwhile Nancy had hurried into the living room. Her father was battling another masked intruder in the hall beyond. The man's mask fell off and Nancy caught a glimpse of a cruel face with a set jaw and fiery eyes. He was of medium height and muscular.

Mrs. Merriam was in the hall, crying, "Stop that! Stop that!"

The intruder seemed determined to hurt Mr. Drew, who kept dodging blows but sending back some stinging ones in return.

Mrs. Merriam, seeing Nancy, exclaimed, "What will we do?"

"Run upstairs and call the police!" Nancy directed.

Her father's attacker, apparently having heard Nancy's request, suddenly whirled and made a dash to the front steps.

Mr. Drew was breathing heavily. Nevertheless he started out the door after the intruder.

Nancy grabbed his arm. "Please don't!" she begged. "He may be armed. Let the police handle this!"

She closed the door and picked up the mask which had fallen to the floor. "This may be a clue to yours and Hannah's attackers, Dad," she said, and told of the man in the kitchen.

They hurried there. "He escaped!" Bess cried out.

"I don't understand," the lawyer said, "what those men hoped to accomplish."

"My guess is," Nancy replied, "that they wanted to hurt us so we'd be unable to work on Mrs. Merriam's case."

"What makes you think that?" he asked.

Nancy told her father about the warning she had received over the telephone.

"On the other hand," the lawyer said, "there may be a gang that has a grudge against Willis Basswood."

Although Mr. Drew was upset by what had occurred, he smiled when he heard how George had used her knowledge of judo on Hannah's attacker.

"Good for you," he said. "Can you give a good description of him?"

"Indeed I can," Hannah spoke up indignantly. "I pulled off his mask. He looked like a gorilla!"

Mrs. Merriam had joined the group and said the police were on their way. "I wish someone would explain what the ruckus was all about."

Nancy gave her the phone message and Mr. Drew said, "I think, Mrs. Merriam, you may be right in mistrusting Mr. Basswood. Apparently there's a connection between him and those thugs. You must be very careful from now on."

Police sirens wailed and within seconds two cars

raced up the driveway. Four officers jumped out. Three started to search the grounds while one remained at the front door.

By this time the Drews and their friends had gathered in the living room. The lawyer opened the door and invited the officer inside.

"Which way did your intruder go?" the policeman asked.

"There were two men—one at the front door and one at the back," Mr. Drew replied.

"Who saw which direction the one at the back took?"

Bess and George said that he had gone to the rear of the garden and jumped the hedge. They described him as a strong, heavy-set man with a long scar on his right wrist.

The officer said, "I think we know who he is. It won't be too hard to pick him up. He earns a living as a strong-arm man for underworld characters."

"Oh, how dreadful!" Mrs. Merriam exclaimed.

Nancy described the man who had come in by the front door. The two masks were examined. They were identical.

"Those thugs were working together all right," the officer declared. Then he hurried outside to report to the other men, taking the two masks with him.

"It's all my fault!" Mrs. Merriam berated herself.

She was pale and looked as if she were going to faint. As the woman slumped into a chair, Hannah Gruen hurried off to bring her a cup of tea.

The hot beverage revived Mrs. Merriam. Looking intently at Nancy and her father, she said, "I think you should give up the case."

Nancy was stunned. She was already intrigued by the suspicions against Mr. Basswood. "Besides," she thought, "I haven't heard the story of the whispering statue."

CHAPTER II

Name, Please

Mrs. Merriam's announcement was followed by a long, embarrassing pause. Mr. Drew did not feel that he should urge a new client to go on with the case if she did not wish to. Nancy, Bess, and George looked down at the floor, not knowing what to say.

Their caller must have realized that her remark had stunned the others. She said quickly, "Please don't think I believe you're incapable of handling this matter. I just don't want anybody to get hurt."

Everyone looked at her and smiled. Mr. Drew said, "We're used to this sort of thing, Mrs. Merriam. Don't worry about us. However, I don't want anything to happen to you. You said your husband is away a great deal. I'd advise you not to stay in your house alone."

Nancy added, "And please spend tonight with us, Mrs. Merriam."

The woman smiled gratefully. "You are very kind people. I admit I am a little afraid to go back to Waterford this late. It's a fairly long trip by plane and then I have to drive to my house."

Mr. Drew said, "Indeed you must stay."

The conversation was interrupted by the ringing of the phone. Mr. Drew answered and was told that the police were calling. Chief McGinnis, a long-time friend of the Drews, came on the line. He said, "That man who escaped from your home by the front door has not been apprehended.

"However, we caught that burly fellow who barged in your back door. He refuses to give his name and claims he is innocent." The chief chuckled. "He had the nerve to say that Mrs. Gruen had attacked him!"

"How did he explain the mask?" the lawyer asked.

"He didn't. We're checking the fingerprints on both masks."

Mr. Drew reported the conversation to the others. "I imagine the police will keep the fellow in jail until he's willing to cooperate. And now I have a surprise to tell all of you. I know Mrs. Merriam is in a hurry to have this mystery solved. Unfortunately I am busy on another case which will take me out of town for a while.

"If you're willing, Mrs. Merriam, I should like

Nancy, Bess, and George to go to Waterford without me and stay at your yacht club. I can highly recommend my daughter as an amateur sleuth."

Hannah Gruen spoke up. "Nancy has a long list of accomplishments and Bess and George have been a wonderful help to her. She discovered *The Secret of the Old Clock* and recently solved *The Mystery of the Ivory Charm*."

Mrs. Merriam's face broke into a wide smile. "I shall be delighted to work with them. But as I said before, I don't want anyone getting hurt. If you girls promise not to take any chances, I'll say yes."

At once Bess said, "I promise!"

George added that she would see to it Nancy took no unnecessary chances.

Mr. Drew said he had a request of his own. "Nancy, I want you to use a disguise and an assumed name while you're working on this case."

Again Mrs. Merriam looked alarmed. "Is that necessary? Won't it bring more trouble to Nancy?"

The lawyer shook his head. "It should be good protection."

Bess asked, "How did the person on the phone and the two attackers know Mrs. Merriam is here?"

Suddenly the woman put a hand over her mouth and fear came into her eyes. "I'm afraid," she said slowly, "that a friend of mine might have given the whole thing away. I thought she could be trusted to keep a secret. She told me she had been down to Mr. Basswood's art store. She is a great talker and I'm afraid may have mentioned my plans."

Mr. Drew frowned. "That is unfortunate," he said. "I shall not be working on the case, however, so if they follow me they will learn nothing. But if they think Nancy is coming to Waterford, that's a very good reason why she should assume a disguise."

Bess remarked that it was lucky the man who had seen her in the kitchen was in jail. The one in the front hall had not had a glimpse of any of the girls.

There was a slight lull in the conversation as each one in the group thought about the case. The silence was broken by George.

With a broad grin she asked, "Let's work on a new name for Nancy. Since it's a mystery about books, how about Libby, for library—Booker?"

The others laughed.

Bess's eyes began to twinkle. "Mr. Basswood's name is partly fish. How about Nancy calling herself Carrie Fisher?"

Again there was laughter and many suggestions followed. In the end it was Hannah Gruen who proposed a name which appealed to Nancy.

Smiling, Nancy said, "From now on will everyone please address me as Miss Debbie Lynbrook."

"Okay, Debbie," said Bess and George together. Bess added, "I just hope we don't make any mistakes and call you by your own name."

Nancy chuckled. "If you do, I won't pay any attention to you."

Mr. Drew said that he would get in touch with Mr. Ayer, the manager of the yacht club, and tell him what the plan was. He would request that all messages for Nancy Drew be rerouted to Mr. Ayer. The only ones Nancy was to take were those under the name Debbie Lynbrook.

The light turn in the conversation had revived Mrs. Merriam's spirits. Hannah suggested that they now eat her raspberry shortcake. Everyone returned to the table and sat down.

Bess said, "Mrs. Merriam, Nancy hinted that you know something about a whispering statue. Will you tell us the story?"

"I'll be glad to," she replied. With a smile she added, "It concerns the yacht club. Maybe you three girls would like to solve that mystery too."

Mrs. Merriam said that the statue was life-size and of fine Italian marble. It had been imported from Italy many years before by a man who was of Italian descent.

"He lived in the mansion, which is now the Waterford Yacht Club. The statue stood on the front lawn."

Suddenly Mrs. Merriam stared at Nancy. "You

know, as I recall the face of the sculpture, the young woman looked very much like you. Actually, she was supposed to resemble the wife of its owner. The couple had come from Italy, but she never got over a feeling of homesickness. She passed away while still in her twenties."

"How sad!" Bess murmured softly.

Mrs. Merriam said she had never known the woman but had met the husband a few times. "He was a very nice man. He died suddenly and it took a long time to settle the estate. In the meantime the yacht club decided to purchase the place."

Nancy asked, "Was the statue there at that time?"

"Oh yes. It was stolen between the time the contract was signed and the day the yacht club took title to the property. The theft was reported to the police. Though they made a careful investigation, no clues were ever found."

"I should think," said George, "that if the statue whispered, tracing it would be easy."

Hannah Gruen suggested that perhaps the marble figure had been taken away by boat and shipped out of the country.

"That's possible," said Mr. Drew. "Well, you girls are going to have a busy time at Waterford." He asked Mrs. Merriam if she had ever heard the statue whisper.

"Indeed I did. It was kind of weird. Sometimes

you could almost distinguish words. There were warnings and then affectionate little murmurings."

By the time the raspberry shortcake had been eaten, Bess and George said they really should return home. Mr. Drew offered to drive them there. After they had gone, Nancy and Hannah took Mrs. Merriam to the second floor. As they led her into the guest room, she again remarked how kind they all were.

"I can never thank you enough," she said as Hannah pulled out a bureau drawer and showed her where there was a nightgown, robe, and slippers.

Nancy said good night and left the room. Instead of going to her own bedroom, she went back downstairs. She called her little terrier Togo from his special place in the basement. He was an affectionate animal and the Drews had made it a rule that whenever they had guests, he would have to stay downstairs. Nancy sat down in a comfortable upholstered chair in the living room and he jumped into her lap.

As Nancy fondled her pet, and waited for her father's return, she thought about the two mysteries at Waterford.

"It's going to be a real challenge," she decided. "I'll wear a full wig which will cover part of my face. And I'll use some quick tanning lotion to darken my skin."

Mrs. Gruen came downstairs and said she wondered why Mr. Drew had not come back. "It doesn't take this long to get to Bess's and George's homes."

Nancy glanced at her watch and was alarmed to see that it was nearly midnight. Had something happened to her father?

CHAPTER III

The Ambush

HALF an hour later Nancy decided to call the Faynes to see if George was home.

"Good idea," Hannah replied. "If she and Bess aren't home get in touch with the police."

Nancy dialed the Fayne number but could not hear a ring. She put the phone down, then picked it up. There was no dial tone.

"I'm afraid our line is out of order," she told Hannah.

Nancy began to pace the floor while the housekeeper sat in a living-room chair staring straight ahead. Finally she said, "Maybe your father tried to phone here and couldn't reach us."

Nancy nodded. She was alarmed for the safety of her father and the girls because of what had occurred earlier at the house.

Suddenly she stopped pacing. A car was coming up the driveway. Nancy ran to the kitchen and turned on the light.

Her father was home!

She greeted him at the back door. "We were so worried about you, Dad," she said. "Did something happen?"

He smiled. "I've had an interesting adventure," he replied. "Come into the living room and I'll tell you about it."

Nancy and Hannah were not too surprised to learn that the lawyer had been followed when he left the house with Bess and George. "I decided it might be a good idea if the men trailing me didn't know where the girls live, so we all went to a soda shop."

As he paused, Nancy asked, "And then?"

Her father said he was sure friends of Bess and George would be in the shop and glad to take the girls home separately. "If I were followed, I could play a game of hare and hounds and get away."

"And you did?" Hannah Gruen asked.

"Finally," he answered. "By the way, I tried to phone here, but the line was dead."

"I found that out too," Nancy told him. "Dad, were you followed after you left the soda shop?"

"Yes. I thought of dodging through the various streets to lose my pursuers, but decided on a better idea." He chuckled. "My plan worked. The instant the two men in the car tailing mine saw me head for the door of police headquarters, they went down the street so fast I couldn't even get their license number."

"Clever," Hannah remarked. "Well, I'm glad you're here safe and sound. And now I'll say good night."

Nancy and her father remained on the first floor. "Do you suppose," Nancy asked, "that our phone line might have been cut?"

"I'll go out and take a look," her father replied. "I'll be glad when all the phone wires have been put underground. Then this can't happen."

The outside line for the Drews' telephone ran overhead from the street and down the side of the house. The beam of a flashlight revealed that it indeed had been cut.

"The phone company can't repair it until the morning," Mr. Drew told Nancy. "But in the meantime I'll see what kind of electrician I can be. I'll attempt to splice this wire so we can call the police and report what happened."

He was successful, though the connection proved to be scratchy and jumpy. Nevertheless, his message was understood by the sergeant on duty at the headquarters desk.

Then Mr. Drew called the telephone company's repair service department. Early the next morning two men arrived to replace the damaged wire. As soon as they left, Nancy phoned Bess and George.

"I think it would be safer if you don't come here before we leave on our trip. Whoever followed Dad probably got a pretty good look at you girls. We'll meet at the airport tomorrow at ten o'clock. I won't leave the house before going. When we get together again I'll be Miss Debbie Lynbrook. Please don't act surprised."

The cousins agreed to the arrangement and said they could not wait to see Nancy in disguise.

"Are you going to order your wig over the phone?" Bess asked.

"Yes. And I'll have it delivered here."

After breakfast Mr. Drew suggested that Mrs. Merriam not go back to her own home until her husband returned. She agreed to stay with a friend. A short while later a taxi came to take her to the airport.

As she said good-by to the Drews and Hannah Gruen, she again expressed her appreciation for their hospitality, and said she was looking forward to the girls' visit to Waterford.

"I don't believe we should be seen together there," Nancy said.

Regretfully Mrs. Merriam agreed. "But we'll be talking on the phone," she said.

Nancy spent the day packing, writing some letters, and going over the various angles of Mrs. Merriam's mystery. Mrs. Gruen had become very quiet and Nancy knew she was worrying as she always did whenever the young detective took on a new mystery. Finally Nancy put an arm about the housekeeper and smiled.

"If I seem to be running into danger, Bess and George will stop me. Besides that, I promise to be careful."

As she finished speaking, the front doorbell rang. For a second Nancy and Hannah wondered if one of their enemies might be returning. Before opening the door, they peered outside, then both began to laugh. Ned Nickerson was standing there!

Ned was a special friend of Nancy's and dated her whenever he could get away from either college or his part-time summer job of selling insurance. Nancy opened the door.

"Hi!" she said as he stepped inside.

Seeing a look of relief in her eyes as well as Hannah's, he asked, "Whom were you expecting —a burglar?"

"Yes," Mrs. Gruen replied. "Nancy will tell you about our experiences with a couple of masked intruders."

"What!" exclaimed the tall, handsome football player from Emerson College.

He was amazed to hear about the two mysteries Nancy was about to try solving at Waterford.

"Good night!" he exclaimed. "You sound as if you might need a little male assistance. Don't be surprised if I show up at the yacht club."

Nancy grinned. "Have you lost your insurance job?" she teased.

"Not up to an hour ago," he replied. "But seriously, don't be surprised if I arrive at the yacht club for the weekend."

"Wonderful!" Nancy replied. "Let's make it definite. And how about bringing Burt and Dave with you?"

Burt Eddleton and Dave Evans were friends of George and Bess. They, too, attended Emerson.

"I'll get in touch with them," Ned promised.

Nancy told Ned of her planned disguise and change of name. "Warn the other boys not to give me away," she said. "Would you like to meet Debbie Lynbrook?"

"I thought I was talking to her," Ned replied.

Nancy asked him to sit down in the living room while she put on her disguise. She hurried upstairs and unpacked the wig which had been delivered an hour before. She had applied the tanning lotion early that morning and now dusted dark powder on her face and neck, then adjusted the long black wig, pulling the sides of it over her cheeks. The finishing touch was a pair of horn-rimmed sunglasses.

Walking into the living room, Nancy said in a voice a couple of tones higher than her own, "How do you all like Debbie's hair?"

Ned burst into laughter. "I'd certainly never recognize you. And the voice is perfect. Say, when I come to see you Saturday, do you think I should wear a wig too and change my voice?"

"You stay just the way you are," Nancy replied.

Ned joined the family for dinner but left soon afterward. Nancy went to bed early, eager for the next day when she could start working on the whispering statue mystery and trying to find out more about Willis Basswood.

In the morning she met Bess and George at the airport. The cousins had difficulty keeping their faces straight, especially when Nancy spoke in her assumed voice.

The three girls looked around to see if they were being observed but decided they were not. The plane trip proved to be uneventful. When the jet landed, the girls were the only passengers to alight. The place was almost deserted and there were no taxis.

But presently a man drove up in a station wagon and jumped out. On the front of the cap he wore were the initials WYC.

"You girls going to the yacht club?" he asked.

When they said Yes, he added, "Jump in. I'll put your bags in the back."

The highway ran directly to the oceanfront. Here the driver turned left and drove for some distance. The area was uninhabited and the roads were heavy with sand. After a while the car went up a weed-choked driveway toward a large, weather-beaten house. On the ocean side of it, sand dunes ran down to the water's edge.

As the driver headed straight for the entrance,

George whispered to the other girls, "This is no yacht club!"

"You're right," said Nancy. "We've been tricked! Get out as fast as you can and follow me!"

When the car slowed down, the girls opened the doors and scrambled out. The driver instantly began blowing his horn. As the girls ran down the dunes toward the beach, two men came from the house. The three strangers jumped into a small car nearby and started to give chase, bumping down the hillside.

"Oh, they'll catch us!" Bess wailed.

"We must change our direction," Nancy said quickly. "They won't be able to turn around very fast in this sand."

She headed back up the incline. At once the men leaped from their car and ran after the fleeing girls.

CHAPTER IV

Alias at Work

THE girls had no idea which way to head for safety. One thing was in their favor—the men pursuing them were past middle-age, heavy, and not so agile.

"Where'll we go?" George asked, puffing a bit. "We can't run all the way back to the airport."

"I know," Nancy replied, "and besides, our bags are in that station wagon. I think we'd better head there first and take them out."

The girls sped on. As they reached the rear of the car, they turned to see where their pursuers were. The men were about two hundred yards away!

Nancy was thinking hard. Somehow she must outwit their potential abductors! Spotting the key in the ignition, she cried out, "Girls, jump in!"

"Why?" Bess asked.

"If we try to carry those bags we'll be caught," Nancy replied.

As she slipped behind the wheel, her companions climbed in. She switched on the ignition, turned the car, and roared down the sandy road.

"Sensational!" George cried. "That's using your head!"

Bess looked frightened. Her conscience could not quite approve of Nancy's taking the car, yet she told herself that under the circumstances there was nothing else to do.

Meanwhile George had looked back and was watching the men who stood in the road, anger and bewilderment on their faces.

"You can't outsmart Nancy Drew!" she said as if addressing them. Then she grinned. "Pardon, Debbie Lynbrook. It was *you* who did this."

Nancy made good time back to the airport. Here she telephoned the Waterford Police Department, and spoke to the officer in charge, Captain Turner. He was astounded at her story and said he would send men at once both to the airport and to the mansion.

"Do you know why those men wanted to hold you?" he asked.

"No. I never saw them before and I'm a stranger in Waterford."

Nancy wondered if the three men were part of a gang that had something to do with the Basswood case or the whispering statue mystery. Had they penetrated her disguise? And how had they learned that the girls were arriving?

"Well," said Captain Turner, "I advise you and your friends to watch your step."

"We will," Nancy promised.

Two officers soon arrived at the airport and Nancy handed one of them the keys to the station wagon. He scrutinized the license plate, then said:

"This is a stolen car. It won't help us trace those men, but the owner will be glad to get it back."

The other officer had gone to telephone for a taxi to pick up the girls. The taxi arrived in a few minutes and the girls were driven to the yacht club, which was in the opposite direction to the old mansion.

As they entered the expansive grounds, Bess exclaimed, "What a beautiful place!"

There was a large garden with hedges on three sides. Flower beds were laid out in symmetrical patterns. Roses and delphinium were particularly prominent. At the far end of the grounds stood a long formal-looking Italian-type building of white cement.

When the taxi reached the entrance, two young men in well-fitting blue uniforms took their bags. They led the girls through a tastefully furnished lobby to the registration desk.

Nancy asked for Mr. Ayer, the manager. "Please tell him Debbie Lynbrook is here."

A few moments later the desk clerk took Nancy to Mr. Ayer's private office. She closed the door and shook hands with him.

In a low voice he said, "You're Nancy Drew?"

"Yes. My father sends his greetings and said he would telephone you once in a while to find out how I'm getting along. You know I'm here to solve a mystery for Mrs. Merriam."

"Yes, he told me, and I wish you all the luck in the world."

Nancy did not mention the whispering statue. She would do that later. Right now she wanted to settle the matter of accommodations and take a shower. Her race on the sand dunes to escape the would-be kidnappers had left her feeling pretty disheveled.

She went back to the desk and registered as Debbie Lynbrook. The clerk, whose name was Sam Lever, suggested that the three girls share one bedroom.

"The rooms here are very large. I have a nice one overlooking the bay. It has two double beds."

The girls decided to take it. Upon seeing the room, they were delighted. It not only had a sweeping view of the bay which was a few miles from the ocean, but the decorations were unusually attractive.

After the girls had showered and were changing into slacks and sport shirts, they began to discuss the attempted kidnapping.

George asked, "Do you suppose those men know who we are, or had they just received orders to abduct three girls coming by plane?"

Bess looked at Nancy who once more had put on the wig and dark face powder. "I'm sure they didn't guess you're Nancy Drew," she said. "But they may have found out who George and I are. Oh, I'll never forget those two ugly men that came out of that mansion! I hope I never see them again!"

George grinned. "Don't bet on that. If they have been hired to keep us from solving the Basswood puzzle or the whispering statue mystery, they aren't going to give up easily."

Nancy telephoned police headquarters and asked for Captain Turner.

"This is Debbie Lynbrook, Captain. Have those kidnappers been caught?"

The officer said that unfortunately they had not. "We went to the mansion and found it deserted, though we did see some rope and several men's handkerchiefs which might have been intended as gags. I think you were right that the men planned to hold you girls there. But I want to assure you that all the police in surrounding towns have been alerted. If you feel, however, that you need our personal protection, please phone me."

Nancy promised to do this and said goodby.

The girls ate lunch, then went back to their room. Bess stood at the window, taking deep breaths of the clear salt air. "Let's forget those horrible men," she said, "and stroll down to that heavenly-looking beach in our swimsuits. I see a lot of boats."

Within minutes the girls were running barefoot along the sand, playing tag with the breaking wavelets. Nancy was dangling a bathing cap in her hand.

"I'm glad it's calm," George remarked. "Say, maybe we could use one of those sailboats!"

There were a variety of boats tied up—small sailing dinghies, rowboats, Boston Whalers. Larger sailboats were moored offshore. Several Sailfish had been pulled up on the beach.

"I'd rather take the Boston Whaler," said Bess. "It's fast and easy to handle. I hate to be at the mercy of the wind, especially if those men try to catch us again," she added, shivering in spite of the hot sun.

"I don't think the attendant would let us," Nancy replied. "At least not without checking us out. I wonder where he is."

"Oh, come on. Let's sail," George urged impatiently.

"There's a sign by that boat," Nancy said, pointing to a flat-hulled racer. "Maybe it will clue us in on the rules."

The girls read the sign carefully. Guests of the

yacht club were allowed to take out the Sailfish, dinghies, and rowboats at any time. Permission to use the Boston Whaler and the larger sailboats had to be obtained from the attendant. But he was temporarily off duty.

"Let's each take a Sailfish and have a race," George cried, running over to a pretty light-blue boat, with a yellow sail wrapped neatly around the mast. The mast and rudder had been placed carefully next to the hull.

"That sounds like fun," Nancy said enthusiastically. "Which boat would you like, Bess?"

Nancy was eying a dark-green one with a red stripe around it. Its white sail, mast, and rudder were placed exactly like the others.

"Someone keeps things shipshape around here," she thought admiringly. "These boats look like painted wooden soldiers all lined up."

"I'll stick to the rowboat, thanks," Bess said. "I'd rather be under my own steam. If I took a sailboat, the wind might blow me somewhere I didn't want to go," she added, glancing at a breakwater of rocks not far away.

"Don't worry, Bess," said Nancy. "Why don't you come with me? We can always tack back when you say the word. It's a light offshore wind," she added, looking up at the pennant on the boathouse. "And I promise to head up into the wind, whenever you're scared, although I don't relish getting in irons. Oh well, if we do, you can jump out and push!" Nancy laughed.

"Thanks," Bess answered.

"Why don't you all go together in the Wee Scot?" said a deep voice.

The girls wheeled around in surprise. The speaker was a smiling attractive young man.

"Who's he?" asked Bess.

"Who's who?" the young man queried.

"Wee Scot," Bess answered indignantly. The others chuckled.

"Wee Scot is the name of a class of racing sailboats," the stranger explained. Pointing to the harbor, he said, "That white, fifteen-foot, sloop-rigged boat moored out there is one."

Nancy turned to the young man. "We'd love to try her, but the sign says that we can use only the Sailfish unless we get permission from the attendant."

"That's me—Dick Milton, the attendant, and you have my permission. From what I overheard, sounds as if you know what you're doing. Come on into the boathouse and get her bag of sails. If you like the feel of her you might enter the race here Saturday afternoon."

Soon the girls were in the dinghy rowing out to the Wee Scot named *Top Job*. Nancy had carefully covered her wig with a large bathing cap and firmly strapped it under her chin.

"What a bore this is," she complained, tugging at the tight strap. "I hate bathing caps!"

"It's better than catching your wig in the rigging or losing it overboard," George remarked. "Then we would be in a spot. I don't think Bess and I could do much mystery solving without you."

Nancy laughed. "Oh sure you could."

"I hope the name of this boat is prophetic," Bess said.

Once aboard *Top Job*, George and Nancy had the mainsail and jib up in record time. Bess dutifully coiled the sheets.

"The wind is perfect." George sighed happily, taking the tiller.

Top Job sailed smoothly, gathering speed as the sails filled. The boat was running before the wind. As the craft approached the mouth of the harbor, George noticed a post she assumed was a racing marker. She decided to have a look at it, thinking she might take part in Saturday's races.

"Ready about, hard alee!" she called.

Nancy uncleated the jib sheet. Then she and Bess scrambled to the other side of the boat. Nancy trimmed the jib sheet, cleating it on the starboard side. George handed her the tiller, saying, "Try her. She handles beautifully."

Bess did not appear happy. "Ugh, see all those messed-up ropes—I mean sheets," she groaned, straightening them out again.

"The wind's freshening," Nancy remarked as the boat, picking up speed, began to heel over. "This is fun."

"It's getting so dark," Bess said apprehensively, looking at the sky.

"That's strange," thought Nancy. "It is dark and feels as if the wind's changing." Glancing at the pennant on top of the mast, she saw in dismay that the wind had shifted abruptly. Suddenly she yelled:

"Jibing over!"

The boom swung across with a bang. George ducked, but the spar hit Bess, throwing her into the water.

"Bess! Bess! Are you all right?" George screamed.

Nancy tried to steady the boat and tack away from the marker which she saw was made of concrete. In a moment the boat scraped hard against it and began to take in water.

"Here we go!" she cried as *Top Job* slowly capsized.

CHAPTER V

An Amazing Find

NANCY, Bess, and George clawed their way to the surface. Bess had a red mark on her cheek, but said she was all right. To the girls' amazement the wind had died down.

"That was a freak blow," said Nancy.

"What did we hit?" Bess asked. Her question was answered as the girls looked at the concrete marker on which a warning was painted in red: *Danger. Sunken schooner.*

Quickly they righted the sailboat. But it was shipping water fast from the gouge in her side.

"It'll sink!" Bess cried.

Nancy did not comment. Instead she looked under the deck, hoping to find extra rope so they could lash the sailboat to the post. To her relief she discovered a coil of rope, together with a heavy sweater.

"Here, girls," she called, tossing the rope to them. "Try to tie *Top Job* to the post."

Bess reached up to catch the rope but her chilled fingers missed it.

"Oh!" she cried out.

"Never mind," said Nancy.

She had succeeded in cramming the sweater into the hole. Now she dived to locate the rope. Nancy could not see it and had to surface.

"I'll go down," George offered. But she too met with failure.

Bess took a turn but came up empty-handed. The three girls went down again and again, but rose to the surface, panting, and had to rest for a few moments before submerging again.

Once, when they came up, Bess remarked, "I think it's hopeless. There's a lot of mud down there." Soon George also gave up but Nancy was persistent.

"One more dive," she said. "Then I'll quit too."

This time her groping hands found the rope on the deck of the schooner. Her lungs almost bursting, she made her way to the top of the water.

As she grabbed the marker, Bess cried out, "You found it!"

She and George took the rope and secured the mast of the sailboat to the marker.

Bess was concerned about Nancy, who was shivering. "Are you all right?" she inquired.

"I'll be okay in a few minutes," she replied, "The old lungs took a beating."

George declared that hereafter when they went sailing they should carry skin-diving equipment with them. The next second she cried out, "Oh, here comes somebody in a Boston Whaler!"

To the girls' delight the newcomer was Dick. "Gee, I'm sorry," he said. "When that sudden blow came up, I figured you might have some trouble."

"You're a real lifesaver, Dick!" Bess exclaimed gratefully.

The girls pulled themselves into the Whaler while Dick anchored the sailboat. When he learned of Nancy's determination to save the craft, he shook his head in disbelief.

"Boy, you're something!" he said. "I don't think I'd have had the courage to try it."

Nancy smiled. "Do me a big favor, Dick. Promise you won't tell a single soul about this."

"Okay, Debbie. I'll have to report what happened to the sailboat, of course, but I'll keep your brave deed a secret."

"Thanks," Nancy murmured.

Dick added, "Don't feel bad about this. Even the best sailors have accidents. Frankly I don't think the repair job on this Wee Scot will be expensive."

Nancy insisted she would pay for any damage and Dick replied, "We'll see about that."

When the girls reached the yacht club, Nancy quickly changed into a pink sports dress, and then went to Mr. Ayer's office. She told him about the accident to the sailboat and insisted upon reimbursing the yacht club for necessary repairs.

The manager smiled. "I see that your adventures in Waterford have already started."

"I hope the others will have a happier ending," Nancy replied. "Mr. Ayer, I've heard about the whispering statue that was stolen from here. Where did it stand?"

He said that it had been in the center of the narrow lawn at the front of the club facing the bay.

"Were there any clues to the thieves?" the young detective queried.

"None whatever. I have the feeling that the police gave up in despair trying to find the thieves and the statue."

Mr. Ayer said he himself had never seen the marble figure, since he had not come to the club until a year ago when it was ready to open.

"I'm told the statue was very beautiful. Do you know the story about it?"

Nancy repeated what Mrs. Merriam had said: that the statue looked like the wife of the original owner of the property, that she never overcame her homesickness for her native land Italy, and that she had died while in her twenties.

"Mr. Ayer, did you ever hear any theories on why the statue whispered?"

"No, I never have." He chuckled. "Do you intend to try finding the marble lady?"

"Yes, although I have another job to do for my father. But I'd like to see the exact spot where the statue stood. Would you mind showing it to me?"

"Not at all."

He led the way to the front lawn and pointed to an oversized flower urn containing petunias. "We covered the spot with this," he said, "but I suppose it's a poor substitute for a beautiful marble piece. The whispering statue would be a great addition to the yacht club. I wish you luck in trying to find it."

As the manager excused himself to go back to his office, Bess and George joined Nancy. She told them what she had just learned and suggested that the girls make a thorough search of the area.

The three friends separated and began a minute hunt for any telltale clues to the thief or thieves. Presently Bess came across part of a torn letter under a stone, but it proved to be only an advertisement. Neither Nancy nor George found any clues. Finally the searchers met in the flower garden.

"I wonder who owns that land on the other side of the hedge," Nancy remarked. "Let's take a look over there."

The girls walked to the far side of the garden and pushed their way through the tightly grown hedge. Just beyond stood a small building which they surmised had been used as a tool house. They headed for it. Finding the door unlocked, Nancy pulled it open. The hinges squeaked loudly.

"Ugh, cobwebs!" said Bess.

The place was cluttered with broken tools and garden equipment, some of it piled on top of other broken pieces.

"Surely," Bess remarked, "you don't expect to find a clue here."

Nancy did not reply. Her keen eyes had detected something long and white propped in one corner and almost hidden by the debris. Pushing objects aside, Nancy made her way toward the corner.

"Girls, this looks like a statue!" she exclaimed.

Bess and George stepped forward and uncovered a dusty marble figure. Hardly daring to believe they had found the missing statue, they carefully turned the sculpture around. It was the life-size figure of a young woman.

"It looks like you, Nancy!" Bess cried out.

Nancy pulled off her wig and the cousins stared first at her, then at the statue. "It certainly does!" Bess added.

"This must be the whispering statue!" George added. "Only it isn't whispering."

"Maybe," said Bess, "if we clean off all this dust, it will whisper!"

After staring at the marble piece, Nancy put her wig back on and said, "We are just guessing this is the stolen statue. The only person we know who can identify it is Mrs. Merriam. Let's go tell Mr. Ayer about our discovery and then phone Mrs. Merriam to come over and look at the statue."

On the way to the yacht club the girls excitedly discussed their amazing find. "So it wasn't really stolen, after all," Bess remarked. "But why would anybody hide the statue in that shed? And why didn't the police find it?"

George suggested that possibly the thieves had not been able to sell the piece and had returned it rather than be caught with stolen property.

"If so," said Nancy, "that must have happened after the police searched the area. The thieves probably were nearly caught when returning the statue and hid it in the shed."

Mr. Ayer was astounded at the girls' news and immediately went with them to the shed. The manager said he would telephone Mrs. Merriam and ask her to come over. Fortunately he found her at home with her husband and the woman promised to drive to the club at once. Nancy suggested that she, Bess, and George go out on the beach during the woman's visit, since they were not supposed to be seen in her company.

"I understand," the manager said. "After she

"It looks like you, Nancy!" Bess cried out

leaves, I'll come to the beach and tell you what she had to say."

The girls took a long walk along the sandy shore. As they returned to the area where the boats were docked, they saw Mr. Ayer coming in their direction. He was smiling.

"Good news for you young detectives," he said. "Mrs. Merriam positively identified the marble piece in the shed as the whispering statue. I've already ordered workmen to give it a thorough cleaning, then to bring it over to the club. The big flower urn on the front lawn will be removed and the statue set in its original place."

"Well, I'm glad that mystery is solved," said Bess. "Aren't you, Nancy?"

Her friend did not reply at once. Finally she said, "I wonder if it really has been solved."

"What do you mean?" Bess asked.

Nancy said, "I won't be satisfied until I hear the statue whisper."

By the time the girls reached the shed, two workmen had brought the marble figure outside and were now loading it into the back of the club truck onto an old mattress. The girls were invited to go along and help steady the statue. The marble figure was taken to the area where cars were washed and given a bath.

"She looks much better," George remarked, "but still she doesn't whisper."

The sculpture was taken to the front lawn and

set in place, so that the young woman looked directly out over the bay. Still there was not a sound from her.

Bess asked, "Is she turned so she's facing exactly toward Italy? I'm sure she did originally."

"I dunno," said one of the workmen. "Which way is Italy?"

No one in the group was quite sure so the statue was turned inch by inch. After a complete semicircle, there was still not a sound from the marble lady.

"What difference does it make?" one of the workmen asked. "She's a beauty and sure looks nice in front of the yacht club."

The girls agreed, then walked off slowly and went to their bedroom to change for dinner.

"Nancy, you've been so quiet," Bess remarked. "What's on your mind? Do you suspect that someone has tampered with the statue and that's why it no longer whispers?"

CHAPTER VI

Thieves

"It's very possible that someone tampered with the statue," Nancy answered Bess's query. "And now she won't whisper. It's up to us to find out what happened."

"Maybe," George spoke up, "the statue never really whispered. The whole story could have been made up to scare people away from this place when it was an estate."

Nancy stood by the window staring down at the marble piece. "You girls are going to be shocked at my guess."

"Just the same I want to hear it," said George.

She and Bess joined Nancy at the window and looked down at the statue. Nancy put an arm around each girl and said, "I have a strong hunch that the statue we're looking at is a reproduction of the original."

"What!" Bess cried. "But why would the thief go to all that trouble?"

"I see Nancy's point," said George. "The thief hoped to fool the police and keep them off his trail."

Bess stepped back and looked at Nancy admiringly. "Your hunches are so often right it startles me. How do you propose to go about proving this one?"

Nancy said she would telephone her father and tell him her suspicions. "He'll know an expert who can give the answer."

Bess and George were amazed at Nancy's deduction. George said, "If you're right, then the thief is a clever person."

Nancy nodded. "And he won't be easy to catch. I believe that the person who made the mold for the reproduction accidentally covered whatever it was that caused the statue to whisper."

"I see what you mean," Bess spoke up. "The police were looking for a statue that whispered."

"I suggest," said Nancy, "that we say nothing about my hunch to anyone except Dad. The thief will think he's safe." She smiled. "He may just get careless and be more easily picked up."

The girls went down to dinner. Nancy telephoned home but no one answered.

The next morning Bess went to their bedroom window to look at the view. Suddenly she cried out and pointed toward the statue. "Those men are moving the marble statue!"

"I wonder if Mr. Ayer knows about this," said George. "Let's find out!"

The girls rushed from the room and downstairs. The manager was not around, so Nancy asked the desk clerk, Mr. Carter, if he knew about it.

"No," he said, "but I can't believe those three men would try to steal the statue in broad daylight."

He requested his assistant to take over and hurried outdoors with the girls. Mr. Carter asked the men why they were moving the piece.

"We got orders to cart it away for cleaning," one of them replied, and the men went on with their work.

"Who at the club gave you permission to take it?" Nancy inquired.

"Nobody. Here's our orders." The mover took an order form from his pocket. It contained no firm's name and neither did the truck, so Nancy asked what company the men worked for.

The man who seemed to be in charge did not reply. He became surly and said, "I don't have to answer questions. Come on, boys. Let's get going."

Mr. Carter's eyes blazed. "Leave that statue alone! You'll have to show better identification before you move it."

One of the other men spoke up. "Come on, Al. We don't want no trouble."

Apparently Al thought so too and the three men went off in their truck.

Mr. Carter turned to Nancy. "Miss Lynbrook," he said, "I believe you girls stopped a robbery just in time."

His statement was confirmed a few minutes later when Mr. Ayer joined them. After being told what had happened, he said, "The club didn't order the statue cleaned. Those men were fakes! I shall have it cemented down to avoid further trouble."

The girls looked at one another. Who wanted the figure removed and why? As they walked into the clubhouse, George asked what the program for the day would be. "I hope it'll be exciting."

"I think," Nancy replied, "that until I can contact Dad—he's out of town—we'd better concentrate on the other mystery."

"You mean Mr. Basswood?" Bess asked.

"Yes." Nancy suggested that the girls visit his art gallery and bookshop.

"All right," Bess agreed. "But you know I couldn't afford to buy anything in the place. What excuse would we have for going in?"

George looked at her cousin a bit scornfully. "When you shop for a dress, do you take the first one you see in the first shop?"

Bess winced. As a shopper, she had the reputation of finding it difficult to make up her mind about any purchase.

Nancy laughed. "You girls will be surprised at what I'm going to ask Mr. Basswood."

"What is it?" Bess queried.

Nancy shook her head teasingly. "I want you to be surprised. We'd better hurry. He may close for an early lunch."

The Basswood Art and Bookshop was very attractive. Statuary and porcelain displayed in the windows were exquisite. Nancy opened the door and the trio walked in. They were in a small hallway with rooms opening off either side and a passageway at the rear. Before they had a chance to notice anything else, they were confronted by a tall slender man. Deep creases in his forehead were an indication that he scowled a great deal.

"Good morning," he said in a crisp voice. "Will you please register in this book." He pointed to an open guest book. "Your names and home addresses."

The girls were taken aback. This was the last thing in the world they wanted to do! Bess and George looked to Nancy for an answer.

Nancy appeared nonchalant. She said with a smile. "Oh, we won't need any catalogs."

The man did not smile back. "It is a rule of Mr. Basswood. I am Mr. Atkin, his assistant."

He picked up the pen and handed it to Bess.

Nancy gave a slight go-ahead nod and Bess signed her name and River Heights address.

George was next. As she gave the pen to Nancy, she fervently hoped that the young detective would not forget she was using an alias. To her delight Nancy put down Debbie Lynbrook, River Heights.

Mr. Atkin glanced at the signatures, then lifted his eyebrows. "You're all from River Heights?" he asked. "Do you know a Miss Nancy Drew who lives there?"

The girls managed to show no surprise and George replied quickly, "I guess everybody in town knows Nancy Drew. Are you acquainted with her?"

The girls were curious when he answered, "Not personally, but a client of mine from River Heights has spoken of her."

"Oh really?" Bess remarked. "I wonder if we know this person. Would you mind telling us who it is?"

"Mrs. Worth. Are you acquainted with her?"

"Not really," Bess answered. "But we know of her."

The girls did indeed know of Mrs. Worth. She was wealthy, overbearing, and a great gossip. She had, no doubt, followed Nancy's exploits as an amateur detective.

At that moment a slender dark-haired man with

long sideburns came from a room off the hallway marked *Office*. The assistant introduced him as Mr. Basswood.

As the shop owner asked graciously if he could help the girls, Nancy found it hard to believe that he was deliberately cheating Mrs. Merriam.

In her disguised voice, Debbie Lynbrook asked, "May we look around? You have so many beautiful things here it will be hard to decide what to buy."

The two men followed the girls closely as they wandered about, exclaiming over beautiful porcelain objects and fine old paintings. Nancy was fascinated by the lovely statuettes, but when she picked one up and looked at the price, she was astonished.

"I'd have to be very wealthy to buy it!" she said to herself.

Mr. Atkin had gone to the front door and was requesting a stout woman to sign the register. After doing so, the customer went directly to the rare books section. Nancy herself was looking over the collection. The customer paid no attention to Mr. Basswood and instead addressed herself to Nancy.

"I can't decide between this green leather volume and the red-and-gold one."

Nancy wondered if the woman was buying the volume for the cover or the contents. She asked, "Do you like poetry?"

The stout woman giggled. "Only if it's about love."

Nancy examined the two books. The red- and gold-covered volume was in Old English dialect. She was sure the woman would not be able to read it. The green volume, she discovered, did have some love poems.

"I think you'd like this one," she said, handing it over.

"Very well. I'll buy it. Would you mind wrapping it for me?"

Nancy smiled. "I think Mr. Basswood will want to do that." She beckoned him to come forward.

He was just in time to hear the stout woman say, "Oh, salesmen make me nervous. I much prefer women clerks." Nevertheless, the customer trotted off after Mr. Basswood.

Nancy continued to examine the rare volumes. She hoped one of them might contain the name Merriam written inside but none did.

Suddenly a male voice said, "Can you help me? I'm looking for a small painting to give my wife for our twenty-fifth wedding anniversary."

Nancy caught Mr. Basswood looking at her out of the corner of his eye. Apparently he wondered what she would say. She decided to take a chance on making the sale for him.

"How about that one on the wall over there?" she suggested. "It's a cheerful scene of the Mediterranean and has a beautiful silver frame."

"You're absolutely right. I like your taste." He walked over, looked at the price, and said he would buy it.

Nancy directed him to Mr. Basswood. Bess and George, having overheard everything, were amused. They told Nancy they had found nothing they could afford.

Bess asked, "Are you ready to go?"

"In a minute. I want to speak to Mr. Basswood." When he came up to the girls, Nancy said, "Mr. Basswood, I'm staying at the yacht club. It's rather expensive. I'd love to earn money toward my bill. Could you possibly give me a job here?"

CHAPTER VII

Four Spies

FOR a moment Mr. Basswood stared in amazement at Nancy. Then his look of surprise vanished and he asked, "Where have you worked before?"

"Oh no place. But I go to art school and I do know a good bit about paintings."

"And how about statuary?" the shop owner asked.

"Very little," Nancy admitted. "But if you have a catalog, I could study it."

Mr. Atkin had walked up. He had overheard the conversation and now looked even more unpleasant than he had before. He said nothing, however.

Mr. Basswood asked Nancy, "What do you know about rare books?"

"Not much," she said, then gave him a broad smile. "But I did manage to sell a book and a painting."

"Yes, you did," Mr. Basswood admitted. "Furthermore, I've been thinking about what the stout lady said—that salesmen make her nervous. She prefers women clerks."

"I'm sure I could do the job," Nancy told him.

The shop owner thought over the proposition for a full fifteen seconds, then said, "All right, I'll give you a chance. But remember, I'm not making any promise to keep you, and I'll pay you only the minimum wage rate."

Nancy was fearful that he might ask her for a social security number or other type of identification but he said nothing about it and she bubbled eagerly, "How soon may I start?"

"You may come in tomorrow," Mr. Basswood replied. "Your hours will be from ten to twelve and two to four."

"Oh thank you! Thanks very much," said Nancy and the girls hurried off.

It was not until they were two blocks away from the art shop that the three friends burst into laughter.

George remarked, "Debbie Lynbrook, you certainly put that one over. You'd better be a good salesgirl if you hope to stay at the shop and do any sleuthing."

Bess suddenly sobered. "At first I thought all this was funny, but now I'm afraid you're headed for trouble."

"I hope not," the young detective replied. "But it's my only chance to find out what's happening to Mrs. Merriam's rare book collection."

As the girls strolled along, George said, "Will you excuse me for a little while? I have an errand to do. I'll meet you two at the nice soda shop over on that corner."

She went down a side street and Bess said, "I wonder what she's coming up with now."

Nancy and Bess went into the sweetshop to idle away the time. They purchased magazines, a newspaper, and salted peanuts. Then they sat down at the counter to order lunch.

George came in. She said nothing about her errand and Nancy and Bess were a bit curious, because George was not usually secretive. She ordered a soda and a sandwich. As soon as the girls had finished, they headed for the bus station where they had been told there was usually a taxi.

It was not until the three were seated in the taxi that George divulged where she had gone. She took a small package from her purse and put it into Nancy's lap.

"This should help you keep your disguise," she whispered.

Curious, Nancy opened the package. Inside was a stack of calling cards on which had been printed "Miss Debbie Lynbrook."

"How clever!" Nancy said. "Indeed they will

be a big help." Her eyes twinkled. "Tomorrow morning I shall leave one on the table near Mr. Basswood's office."

When the girls reached the yacht club, Bess found a note in her mailbox saying she was to telephone her home at once. She went off to make the call but returned in a few minutes.

"Is everything all right?" George asked her.

Bess replied that she was not sure. "Mother said that Mrs. Gruen phoned and asked her to get this message to Nancy. Some man who refused to give his name called your house several times demanding to talk to you or be told where to find you. Hannah decided not to call you direct."

"He wouldn't give his name?" George asked.

"No, and this worried Hannah. She requested him to give her a number that Nancy could call but he refused."

Bess said the man had been so persistent that Hannah finally had become angry and told him if he would not give his name he should never call again.

"Oh, Nancy, I'm worried too," Bess added. "Your enemies are determined to find you."

Nancy was silent for several seconds, then she smiled slightly. "Do you realize, girls, that this means they don't know where I am, or that I'm Debbie Lynbrook?"

Hearing this, Bess and George relaxed, but advised Nancy to be on the alert for trouble.

"Especially while you're at work," George added.

That evening Nancy telephoned her father. He was amazed to hear about the discovery of the statue and said he would have an expert from New York City examine it.

"It will be interesting to find out whether or not your suspicions about it are correct," the lawyer said.

Nancy then told her father of her job at Basswood's Art and Bookshop. He laughed and wished her luck. But he warned her not to take any chances on the owner discovering she was Nancy Drew.

His daughter chuckled. "Debbie will do her best."

The following morning Bess and George wished the young detective luck. They promised to drop into the shop later to see how she was getting along.

"Let's have lunch in town," Nancy suggested. "I have two hours off."

During the morning Nancy made three very good sales and Mr. Basswood seemed pleased. His assistant, who never changed his expression, kept a sharp eye on her. She began to wonder whether perhaps it was Mr. Atkin and not Mr. Basswood who might be guilty of falsifying Mrs. Merriam's account.

About eleven o'clock a young man came in,

signed the register, and went straight to the book section. Nancy was waiting on a woman interested in paintings and for a few minutes no one was in the book department. While Nancy's customer was trying to make up her mind about an old English landscape, the girl detective saw the young man slip a book into his pocket.

"He means to steal it!" she told herself. "And that's a rare volume!"

Excusing herself to the woman, Nancy hurried to the entrance hall where Mr. Atkin was standing. She whispered her suspicions to him, but he told her he could do nothing.

"If you're wrong, Mr. Basswood could be sued." He turned away.

Nancy was not satisfied. She decided to do something else. She walked casually to the register to get the name of the young man and found it was Sam Payne. She wrote on the card:

I saw Mr. Sam Payne put an early edition of Browning's poems into his pocket.

She looked around for Mr. Basswood but he was not in sight, so she went back to her customer.

"I know I'm taking a long time," the woman said. "But after all, when one spends this much money, one should be absolutely sure."

Just then the front door opened and to Nancy's

delight she saw a police officer come in. She hurried over to him and put the card into his hand. She whispered, "Mr. Atkin won't do anything about it."

The police officer walked toward Mr. Payne. Upon seeing him, the young man made a beeline for the front door. He opened it and hurried outside. The officer followed.

Mr. Payne did not get far. The policeman stopped him and said something which Nancy, who was standing in the doorway, did not hear. Mr. Atkin was also watching the scene.

The young man pulled the stolen volume from his pocket and handed it to the policeman. "I was only holding it until I made up my mind."

Nancy doubted that this was true and wondered what was going through Mr. Atkin's mind. He made no comment when the policeman handed the book to him.

The frozen expression on Mr. Atkin's face remained as the officer said, "You can thank this young lady for retrieving that rare volume for you. Do you want to prefer a charge against this man?"

"Mr. Basswood will have to do that," Atkin replied.

He made no further comment and marched back to the shelf to return the book to its place. The officer looked amazed but merely shrugged and shook his head. He gave Nancy a big smile as he went off with the suspect. She returned to her customer and sold a painting.

At lunch Nancy told Bess and George what had happened. The cousins exchanged glances and Bess said, "I was so worried about you I asked that policeman to drop in."

"Good thing you did," said Nancy.

During the afternoon she made several sales to summer visitors in Waterford. To her chagrin Mr. Basswood told her at four o'clock that she was not to report for work the following morning. But she was relieved when he added that she should come at two o'clock.

In talking this over later with the girls, Nancy remarked, "I think something fishy will be going on at the shop tomorrow morning. Let's get Dick and go down there this evening. Maybe we can spy on the place and learn something."

Dick was delighted with the idea and drove the girls downtown in his small car. Nancy had decided to take him into her confidence, without revealing her identity, and said that certain things happening at the shop made her wonder if the business was being carried on honestly.

The good-looking young man grinned. "I've never tried solving a mystery, but it sounds like fun!"

He parked the car some distance from the shop

and suggested they approach Basswood's from the rear along a driveway.

As they neared the building, Bess whispered, "I see a light in the basement window."

The young people tiptoed forward. They could hear men talking. As they drew closer, Nancy recognized the voices as those of Mr. Basswood and Mr. Atkin.

Reaching the lighted window, the four spies found it wide open. They could see the two men clearly. They were packing books in cartons. Dick hunkered down and stared intently at the scene below.

Mr. Atkin spoke up. "It's a good thing you're getting the rest of this Merriam collection out of here. I don't trust that Lynbrook girl!"

The remark made Bess shiver. She was sure Nancy would be in danger if she went back to work at the shop!

Just then the young people heard a car. They did not want to be caught spying! The girls started to move away. But Dick, startled by the automobile, suddenly lost his balance and tumbled into the cellar of the art shop!

CHAPTER VIII

The Race

THE three girls were aghast when Dick fell through the open cellar window of Basswood's shop.

"What'll we do?" George asked.

"We'd better run!" Bess replied promptly. "Come on!"

Nancy had stretched out her arms to push the cousins away from the window in case the men looked up. In a moment, however, she inched forward and peered down. If Dick had been hurt, she would certainly go to help him!

"But if he's all right," she said to herself, "Bess and George and I had better get away from here as quickly as possible."

Dick had landed on a pile of newspapers evidently used for packing books. When the two men heard the thud they turned quickly. Dick stood up and looked at them sheepishly. He gave no explanation of his sudden entrance.

"He's all right," Nancy thought. "I'm sure he can get out of this predicament himself."

She told this to the other girls and the three scooted away.

"Where shall we wait for Dick?" George asked.

"I vote for the soda shop," Bess said.

Nancy remarked that it was possible when Dick did not see them around, he would figure they had gone back to the yacht club. "Then we'd miss a ride home."

"I guess you're right," Bess conceded. "But a soda sure would taste good right now."

The girls went directly to the parking lot where Dick had left his car. They climbed in.

Ten minutes later he appeared. "Hi! I thought I'd find you here."

As he swung himself into the driver's seat, Nancy said, "Tell us what happened. How did you get away from Basswood and Atkin?"

The young man grinned. "Mostly by keeping still. They asked me what I was doing at the window, and I just shrugged. Then they tried to find out what I had overheard. Again I shrugged. 'Nothing important,' I told them."

As Dick paused, George begged him to go on. "You haven't told us yet how you got away from Mr. Basswood."

"That older man finally said to me, 'I guess you thought we were burglars.' I just laughed and they took it for granted that he had hit upon the truth. The other man told me to go out the way I had come in. Then they slammed the window shut and locked it."

The three girls laughed and Dick asked, "What kind of a detective would I make?"

"Excellent," Nancy replied.

"Then maybe that's what I'll take up when I finish college," the young man said.

As they neared the yacht club, Dick reminded his passengers that the boat races would be held the following day. "Debbie, I hope you can take the afternoon off."

Nancy said she had to work until four o'clock but that she would come directly back to the yacht club. "Ned can pick me up at the shop." She sighed. "I suppose we girls lost our chance to be in any of the races after smashing one of your boats."

"I have a surprise for you," Dick said. "*Top Job* has been repaired and is waiting for you sailors. You can make the last race. Bess and George, you can use it in earlier races. How about it?"

Bess told Dick that she did not plan to enter any of the races, but that George and her friend Burt might take part.

"We'll be there early to get in a little practice," George remarked.

Nancy regretted that Ned would have no time to try out the sailboat, but she consoled herself with the thought, "Winning isn't everything. We'll have a lot of fun and the competition will be great."

When the girls reached their bedroom, Nancy said she had thought of a little scheme. Perhaps she could trap Mr. Basswood!

"Goodness, what is it?" Bess asked.

Nancy said she would call Mrs. Merriam and get the titles of a couple of books on astrophysics which Mr. Basswood was to sell for her. "Then I want Ned to come down to the shop and ask Mr. Basswood if he has the two volumes. There might be a clue in his answer."

She called Mrs. Merriam, who went to consult her list. She came back to the phone and said there were two volumes, *System of the World* by Sir Isaac Newton and *De Orbim Coelestium Revolutionibus* by Nicolaus Copernicus.

"But I'm afraid they've been sold," Mrs. Merriam said. "I was to get ten dollars each as my share."

"Thank you," said Nancy, and told the woman what she planned to do.

"I hope it works." Mrs. Merriam sighed.

Nancy reported what had taken place in the cellar of the shop earlier in the evening, and added, "I'm sure your hunch about Mr. Basswood cheating you is correct."

"I think it's wonderful what you're doing," Mrs. Merriam remarked. "Please keep me posted."

"I will."

The following morning Nancy received a phone call to report for work early. When she rang the shop's doorbell, no one came to answer it. She glanced at her watch. It was five minutes to ten.

For a fleeting second Nancy wondered if no one was there. On a hunch she walked around to the back entrance and peered into the basement. It was dark. She returned to the front of the building and rang again. This time the door was opened by Mr. Atkin. He did not say good morning or make any comment.

Nancy greeted him cheerfully and added, "It's a beautiful day, isn't it? A wonderful day for the yacht club races." Mr. Atkin was still silent.

At that moment Mr. Basswood stepped from his office and remarked that Nancy was very prompt. She replied, "Saturday should be a big one in sales for the shop."

"It usually is. Well, suppose you get to work. Find a dustcloth in the rear room and do some cleaning."

Half an hour later the first customers came in. While Nancy was showing a woman some statuettes, she noticed the front door being opened. Ned Nickerson walked in. He glanced in her direction, but as planned, gave no sign of recognition. She in turn ignored him.

He signed the register, then asked for Mr. Basswood. Mr. Atkin looked a bit annoyed but went to get the shop owner.

"Good morning, sir," Ned said. "I'm interested in astrophysics. I was told to get two certain volumes. Since you deal in rare books, I thought you might happen to have copies. They're Newton's *System of the World* and Copernicus's *De Orbim Coelestium Revolutionibus*."

Nancy heard Mr. Basswood say, "I don't have them here but I can get them for you." He looked Ned up and down as if appraising him as a purchaser of expensive books.

"Great!" Ned said. "How much would they be?"

"Twenty-eight dollars apiece and a bargain at that."

Both Nancy and Ned blinked at this. According to Mrs. Merriam's statement, Mr. Basswood had told her she would get ten dollars apiece. She should receive twenty-one for each!

Nancy was afraid that Ned would say the price was too high and not order the books. She wanted Mrs. Merriam to examine them to see if they had come from her collection. Ned must buy them! Quickly the young detective sidled over to Mr. Basswood.

Ned was saying, "Well, I don't know. That's a lot of money for me to shell out."

Very gently Nancy stepped on one of Ned's toes and hoped he would get the message that he was to pay any price the shop owner asked.

"Are the volumes in good condition?" Ned asked.

"Oh yes," Mr. Basswood replied.

"Then I'll take the books," Ned said. "I'm staying at the yacht club. Please deliver them there when you get them. The money will be waiting at the desk."

Ned glanced around the shop and remarked that the objects for sale were certainly attractive. "But I can't spend any more today." He laughed. "I'm broke after buying those books." He said good-by to Mr. Basswood and left.

Nancy realized she had to give some excuse for having walked up to Mr. Basswood. She said sweetly, "My customer can't seem to make up her mind between two of the statuettes. Perhaps you can point out some things about them I don't know."

Mr. Basswood talked to the woman. He finally helped her make up her mind, but she said, "This was the one the young lady was recommending all along."

The shop owner made no comment and walked off. Nancy worked hard during the day, but promptly at four o'clock she said good-by to Mr.

Basswood and his assistant and hurried away. As prearranged, Ned met her at the town parking lot and they hurried to the yacht club in his car.

"Thanks, Ned, for buying the books. If the ones you receive are from Mrs. Merriam's collection, Mr. Basswood is making a tremendous profit instead of only his commission."

"Wow!"

Nancy dashed into the yacht club to change her clothes and met Ned at the dock. A race was in progress.

Bess and Dave stood there. They said hello to Nancy, and Dave added, "George and Burt are in that leading boat!"

Nancy felt a thrill of excitement. Their craft was tacking in barely ahead of a red one.

Bess began to jump up and down and scream. "George! Burt! Come in! Hurry! Come in!"

Nancy, Ned, and Dave took up the cry. But suddenly their hearts sank. The rival sailboat was pulling ahead! It had caught a freshening breeze at exactly the right angle.

The next second Burt took advantage of the same strong wind and tacked swiftly to starboard. George worked the tiller in perfect harmony and once more the Sailfish shot ahead.

"Come in! Beat 'em!" cried Dave.

The race was a photo finish, but George and Burt were declared the winners.

"You were superb!" Bess exclaimed.

There were congratulations from all sides, then the chairman announced that they were ready for the final race. The contestants scurried to their craft, eager and hopeful. Nancy was to be at the tiller.

As Nancy and Ned took their positions, a boy came running. He called out to the watching crowd, "Telegram for Miss Nancy Drew!"

Instinctively Nancy started to rise, but Ned pulled her back and hissed into her ear, "Sit still, Debbie Lynbrook!"

CHAPTER IX

Foul!

AT Ned's command Nancy quickly sat down in the sailboat. She had nearly given away the show! Playing the part of Debbie Lynbrook was difficult. It was so natural to respond as Nancy Drew!

"I mustn't make another mistake," she thought. "But I wonder who sent the telegram. It probably was a trap. I'm glad I didn't get caught in it!"

On shore Bess and George had heard the messenger call out Nancy's name for a telegram.

"We must do something!" George told her cousin.

Burt and Dave were still discussing the race and had not noticed the boy. Quickly George said to them, "We'll be right back. Wait here!"

Bess followed her as she headed for Mr. Ayer. The yacht club manager had just joined the group on the beach. Quickly George pointed out the messenger and suggested that the manager take the telegram. Then they hurried back to their escorts.

"What's up?" Burt asked.

George whispered an explanation. The four young people watched as Mr. Ayer made his way to the messenger and signed for the telegram. The boy went off.

Boats were approaching the starting line. *Top Job* sailed near the committee boat and Nancy and Ned learned there was to be a one-minute warning gun—and then the start.

"Do you have a stop watch?" Nancy asked him.

"No, but I have a second hand on my watch."

"Good," said Nancy. "How much time do we have?"

The gun sounded and Ned checked his watch. "If you head for the left side of the line, you should just about make it at the gun."

"Do you see George? I wonder about that telegram," Nancy said.

Ned did not reply. Instead he exclaimed, "Nancy, look at that blue boat! It's heading straight at us!"

"I think it'll be okay," said Nancy. "He's on a port tack and we have the right of way."

"Fifteen seconds until the gun," said Ned, looking at his watch.

Nancy leaned forward, watching the blue boat.

"Nancy," warned Ned, "that blue boat is heading straight at us!"

"We'd better warn the skipper," she said. "Starboard tack, starboard tack!" she yelled.

"He has to give way," Ned cried out. But the boat with its two sailors kept coming.

Nancy said under her breath, "I'd better fall off a little and give way."

They veered, missing the blue boat by inches. Ned yelled to the other skipper, "Protest! We're protesting the start!"

The gun roared and Nancy and Ned headed up again and went over the line after the blue boat.

"Looks as if we'll be at the Protest Meeting after the race," said Ned. "I'm going to fly the protest flag."

"Oh, we may win anyway," said Nancy. "I didn't care for their sailing manners, though, and I'm sure they know better. They probably think we won't protest, but we will. It's the right thing to do."

There was a good steady wind. The course was around two buoys and then in. The boats were spread out. Nancy was sailing well and *Top Job* passed the blue boat. It was moving up, though, with two other craft close behind.

As they headed toward the finish line, Ned said, "That guy behind us is putting up the spinnaker, Nancy. Where's ours?"

"Quick! Look under the deck. There's another sail bag there," Nancy replied quickly.

"Nothing here." Ned sighed. "Let's go wing and wing since we're before the wind, and hope for the best."

"We may be better off. Setting a spinnaker is always tricky business," said Nancy. "We'll do well wing and wing, especially since you're crewing."

The blue boat was gaining now, as its spinnaker filled. Nancy and Ned were watching closely. Suddenly the spinnaker began to wobble and Ned yelled, "Look, Nancy, they're in trouble! The spinnaker is fouling around the stay."

The two boats were almost even, but *Top Job* started pulling ahead. The people in the blue craft were obviously anxious and angry.

"They certainly gave us nasty looks," said Nancy. "Guess the wind is too gusty for them to handle."

"They lost their cool—that's all," Ned retorted.

Top Job edged ahead. Ned was working the jib sheets with ease now. The gun sounded and Ned shouted, "We won, we won!"

Nancy grinned. "And without a protest."

"But we could have won more easily if we hadn't been fouled," Ned insisted.

"It doesn't matter," Nancy said. "I think *Top Job* is a nifty little boat."

"I guess so," said Ned, "and you're a nifty little skipper!"

"Thanks," said Nancy, laughing.

The winners were congratulated by the chairman and told that they would be awarded silver trophies later. There was loud applause by Dick and the other onlookers who realized that Nancy and Ned had been fouled at the start.

As the couple walked away, Nancy said, "Now let's find out about that telegram."

She located Bess and George, who told her Mr. Ayer had it. When the excitement over the race had died down, Nancy made her way to the manager's office. As she had suspected, the telegram was indeed a hoax. The sheet inside the envelope was blank!

Nancy smiled. "Whoever sent this did not find out anything," she said. "The trick to make me answer the call didn't work."

Mr. Ayer was visibly disturbed. He asked, "How are you progressing with the case?"

She gave him a brief résumé.

Although pleased with her progress, he admitted being worried. "I'm sure that the person who sent the telegram suspects Nancy Drew is in Waterford. It may be the same man who telephoned your house. If so, he is very determined to find you. I'm alarmed about what he may try next. Nancy, do take every precaution possible."

The young detective nodded, and asked if she might use his office telephone to call Mrs. Merriam. "When Ned's books arrive, I'd like her to come over and examine them to see if they're part of her collection."

Mr. Ayer said he would be very glad to cooperate. "If Mrs. Merriam is willing to drive over here, I'll let her know when the books arrive."

Nancy made the call and the woman said she would be happy to come to the yacht club. She congratulated Nancy that her ruse had worked.

"Of course I may be wrong," Nancy told her, "so don't be surprised if this turns out to be a false lead."

That evening all the guests at the yacht club were invited to participate in an after-dinner gala celebration for the victors in the afternoon races. The recreation room was gaily decorated with purple and pink bunting, the club colors. A peppy band was playing and soon there were many dancers on the floor.

At ten o'clock the drum rolled, the music stopped, and everyone watched as the chairman of the racing committee stepped up to the microphone on the band platform. Two boys carried up a small table on which stood silver cups—the awards to the winners of the races. George and Burt were called forward and each received their prizes. There was loud applause because of the close race they had had.

Debbie Lynbrook and Ned were last. The cups they received were slightly larger and Mr. Ayer mentioned the participants' marvelous sportsmanship in coming in first. Everyone in the room knew they had made no protest about the foul and the clapping was tremendous.

Many people crowded around the couple and congratulated them. "It was a great race," several said.

Nancy was fearful she might be recognized by somebody because she was not wearing her sunglasses. She let her long black hair fall closer around her face, almost covering her cheeks.

"I must get out of here," Nancy thought.

She was relieved when the music began again and she and Ned could dance. As the lights were dimmed, bright moonlight streamed through the windows.

"Let's stroll outside," Ned suggested. "It's a beautiful night."

Nancy was happy to go because she felt very uneasy about possible identification by someone in the club.

"Where would you like to walk?" she asked Ned, gazing out over the calm water in the bay.

"Let's go take a look at the statue," he suggested.

The couple danced to the entrance leading to the front porch. Then they started slowly across the lawn.

The marble figure cast a broad shadow. There was something eerie about the scene with the beautiful young woman looking longingly in the direction of her Italian homeland.

"Too bad the owner's wife was ill and unhappy here," Nancy thought. "The place is so beautiful anyone should find it delightful."

It was very quiet and Nancy and Ned found themselves tiptoeing along and not saying a word. Suddenly Nancy caught Ned's arm and they stopped walking. He looked at her questioningly.

"Ned," she said in a very low tone, "the statue is whispering!"

CHAPTER X

A Near Discovery

NANCY and Ned moved toward the statue quietly, as if their presence might disturb it. The whispered sounds continued.

Finally the couple reached the marble figure and stood listening. A moment later broad smiles spread over their faces. The sounds were not coming from the statue. In fact, it was not whispering at all!

On the other side of the figure a couple sat on the ground, their backs against the sculpture. A young man was saying, "You must marry me. Life is nothing without you."

A girl's trembling voice answered, "I can't! Maybe a year from now when I graduate from college."

Chagrined, Nancy and Ned tiptoed away and returned to the yacht club. There they had a good laugh and Ned remarked, "I wonder how that romance will turn out."

"I guess we'll never know," Nancy replied. "I didn't recognize the voices, so they must be a couple who came here just for the day."

The thought of the statue whispering stayed in Nancy's mind. The following morning after church she and Ned strolled once more to the front of the club to look at the marble lady. A strong wind had come up, so Nancy took a scarf from her pocket and tied it over her wig.

As they neared the statue, Nancy exclaimed, "Listen!"

The two stood still. This time Nancy was not wrong—there were murmuring sounds coming from the marble figure!

"This is remarkable!" Ned exclaimed. "The statue didn't make a sound last night. What do you attribute this to?"

"Two things," Nancy replied. "The wind, for one. And as you know I suspect this is a reproduction. I believe the person who made it came here very late last night and did something to it so that when the wind blows, the statue will make a whispering sound."

"But why should he bother to do that?" Ned questioned.

Nancy said whoever did it hoped to allay any suspicions that the statue was a reproduction.

"I'd like George and the others to hear this," she said.

"I'll get them," Ned offered. "You stay here and see what the young lady has to say."

During his absence the wind died down completely. No sounds came from the statue, but just as the others arrived, the wind suddenly began to blow hard again.

Bess put her ear close to the statue. "I can't believe it!" she said.

George admitted that there were sounds all right, but she could not distinguish any words. "Don't tell me, Bess, that you can make anything out of it."

A slightly frightened look crossed Bess's face. She said, "It sounded as if the statue were murmuring the words, 'Go home! Go home!' "

Dave shook his head. "You certainly have great imagination, Bess."

Nancy examined the statue but could not discover anything different about it.

The three boys looked at their watches and said they must leave directly after dinner. "We'd better eat now," Burt suggested.

The young people went into the club. Nancy stopped to tell Mr. Ayer about their discovery but learned he had gone out to dinner.

While they were eating, Dave said, "Girls, this has been a really groovy weekend. Invite us down again if you need some male help."

"You bet!" George replied. "But I have a hunch Nancy is going to solve this mystery within a few days."

"And that would mean you'd go back to River Heights?" Dave asked.

"I'm afraid so," Nancy replied.

During the afternoon it rained hard and the girls were forced to stay indoors. By the next morning the weather had cleared.

Before Nancy left for work she dropped into Mr. Ayer's office. "Guess what," she said. "The statue is whispering!"

"You're joking!"

"It's true, but only when the wind blows."

"I'll go out and listen. By the way, the books Ned ordered arrived a few minutes ago. I thought you'd want to know."

"Yes, thank you. Shall I get in touch with Mrs. Merriam or will you?"

The manager said he would do it. "Perhaps by the time you get back here, I'll have some news for you."

There were many customers during the morning at the art and bookshop and Nancy was kept very busy. At one point the thought went through her mind, "Mr. Basswood has a wonderful business. He doesn't have to be dishonest. Why should he do anything underhanded?"

Mr. Basswood did little of the selling. He remained in his office, always keeping the door locked. Each time Nancy went to see him, she knocked and he unlocked it. He never let her inside and did not open the door far enough for her to get even a peek at the interior.

"He's certainly secretive and peculiar," she decided.

After she had made her tenth sale of the morning, he gave her a smile and said, "Miss Lynbrook, you are doing a very good job."

Whenever she appeared at the office, he would give her change from his pocket. She was surprised that he carried such a large amount of cash. As Nancy was mulling this over near the book department, she saw a couple come in.

"Oh!" she thought in dismay. "They're Mr. and Mrs. Thompson from River Heights and they know me well!"

While she was debating where she might hide, Mr. Thompson signed the register for the two of them. Nancy decided that she just had time to hurry to the powder room and hide there until the couple left.

But her hopes were dashed when Mrs. Thompson turned in that direction. Her husband came the other way toward Nancy.

Desperate, she jumped behind a life-sized bronze statue of a sailor. As the man moved, she tiptoed around it. All this time she kept one eye out for Mrs. Thompson. Minutes later the woman came into the room and walked toward her husband.

Nancy wondered what to do. She could not hide from both of them! Could she depend on her disguise not to be recognized? In a panic she turned her back on the couple.

"Oh, miss, will you help us?" Mr. Thompson called out.

Instead of replying, Nancy quickly pulled a pad and pencil from her pocket and wrote:

I'm here incognito. Please don't identify me and put this note in your pocket.

She planned to take the Thompsons into her confidence and hoped they would not unwittingly reveal who she was. Surreptitiously Nancy put her hand backward around the side of the statue and the note was taken. There was silence for a couple of moments.

Feeling it was safe now to face the Thompsons, Nancy walked toward them. She held back the two sides of the long hair which partially covered her face. Recognizing her, Mr. Thompson gave the pretty detective a big wink and his wife smiled broadly. They did not call her by name.

Mr. Thompson said he wanted to look over the rare books. His wife was interested in purchasing a statuette.

A few minutes later when neither the owner

nor his assistant was around, Mr. Thompson whispered to Nancy, "Are you on another mystery adventure?"

"Yes. Someday I'll tell you all about it."

She sold the Thompsons two books and a statuette, wrote the sales check, and took the money to Mr. Basswood's office. She knocked on the door but there was no answer.

"He must have gone out," she decided. "I wonder where Mr. Atkin is."

The assistant was not in sight. Since he always stood near the front door when anyone was in the shop, Nancy was puzzled.

She called his name but there was no answer. Nancy walked into the rear room but he was not in it.

"I must leave this money some place!" she thought.

Once more Nancy knocked on the office door. When there was still no response, she tried the knob. To her surprise the door was unlocked.

She opened it wide and walked in. Then she gasped.

Mr. Atkin was slumped over a desk!

CHAPTER XI

Telltale Letter

NANCY was horrified to see that Mr. Atkin was motionless in his chair. The upper part of his body was face down on the desk. She rushed in and immediately felt his pulse. It was extremely faint and intermittent.

"Anyway, he's alive," she murmured. "But I must get help."

She hurried back to Mr. and Mrs. Thompson and told them what had happened.

"Please come," she begged.

They immediately followed her. Mr. Thompson, a physical education teacher, gave the victim a quick examination and said he thought Mr. Atkin had had a heart attack.

"We must get him to the hospital as quickly as possible. Nancy, call the police and get an ambulance here right away."

As she dialed the number, the River Heights couple gently laid the patient on the floor. Mrs. Thompson took some smelling salts from her handbag and tried to revive Mr. Atkin. There was no response.

Nancy by this time was talking to Captain Turner. When she told of her discovery, he said a hospital ambulance would be sent at once to the shop. Within minutes a doctor was giving the victim oxygen.

"He's in bad shape," the doctor said.

During this procedure Nancy had been glancing around the office to learn as much as she could about it. On the desk lay a penciled notation. It read: *M De K 500 on acct.*

Just then Mr. Basswood walked in. He turned pale at the sight. "What happened?" he asked.

Nancy replied, "Apparently Mr. Atkin has had a heart attack. I found the door unlocked and entered. He was slumped across the desk. Mr. and Mrs. Thompson came in to help."

The shop owner gave her a searching look. "This office is private and I don't like any outsiders coming into it!" he said unpleasantly.

The doctor and Mr. and Mrs. Thompson looked at the man in disgust. He did not seem the least bit concerned about the condition of his assistant.

"I'm taking Mr. Atkin to the hospital," the doctor told him.

"Very well. And be quick about it," Mr. Basswood said icily.

A stretcher was brought in, but before Mr. Atkin could be put on it, Mr. Basswood ordered Nancy and the Thompsons out of the office. The instant the victim had been removed, he stepped outside, slammed the door shut, and locked it.

Nancy was shocked by the man's rudeness, but she said calmly, "Mr. Basswood, Mr. and Mrs. Thompson bought two books and a statuette. I left these and the sales slip in your office."

"I'll get them," the shop owner said.

He brought them outside and told Nancy to wrap the two volumes. "I'll attend to the statuette myself," he said, handing the change to Mr. Thompson.

After he had disappeared into the back room, Mrs. Thompson whispered to Nancy, "Don't bother to wrap the books. They're so small they'll fit in my purse. How do you stand it to work for such a man? And why are you here?"

"I can't tell you now." Nancy glanced at her watch. "It's almost lunchtime. Where are you going?"

"To the yacht club."

"Would you mind giving me a ride?" Nancy asked.

"Glad to," Mr. Thompson said.

Presently Mr. Basswood arrived with the statuette. "I noticed from the sales slip that you're from River Heights," he said. "By any chance do you know Carson Drew who lives there with his daughter Nancy?"

Nancy did not show any emotion at the question. She listened intently for her friends' answer.

To her delight Mr. Thompson replied, "Mr. Drew is a prominent lawyer in town. He's well known. I understand his daughter is very attractive."

Mrs. Thompson spoke up. "She has the loveliest golden red hair you ever saw."

Nancy could have hugged both of them but she remained motionless.

She said to the shop owner, "It's twelve o'clock. May I go now?"

"All right. But be back here promptly at two."

He turned and walked away without another word. The Thompsons grinned and shook their heads.

A few minutes later Nancy was in the couple's car and heading toward the yacht club. Mr. Thompson asked Nancy, "What name are you using? I don't want to make a mistake if I happen to see you in the lobby or the dining room."

His question reminded Nancy that she had promised to tell him and his wife about her case. Without going into detail or involving Mr. Basswood directly, she said she was trying to trace a collection of books he had been commissioned to sell. Since he was uncommunicative on the subject, she was hoping to pick up some clues at the shop.

When they reached the club, Bess and George were waiting for Nancy. After she had thanked the Thompsons and introduced them to her friends, Bess drew her aside. "Come into Mr. Ayer's office," she whispered excitedly. "He has some news for you."

The girls excused themselves and hurried off to talk to the manager. He gave Nancy a broad smile. "Miss Lynbrook," he said, "you're certainly on the right track. Mrs. Merriam was here. In one of the books that Ned bought she found a letter which had been written by her uncle to her father but never mailed."

"That's a marvelous clue!" Nancy exclaimed. "There's no doubt that the books are hers."

"It certainly looks," said Mr. Ayer, "as if Mr. Basswood is guilty of fraud."

George spoke up. "What are you going to do—have him arrested?"

Nancy shook her head. "Not until I notify my father. By the way, Mr. Basswood's assistant is in the hospital."

"What!" the others cried.

Nancy told them about Mr. Atkin suffering a heart attack. "I wonder how he is. When I go back to the shop this afternoon, I'll find out."

Bess asked, "When you were in Mr. Basswood's office, did you see anything suspicious?"

"No, but I saw an interesting notation on his desk."

She told about the note saying *M De K 500 on acct.* Nancy asked Mr. Ayer if she might use his phone to get in touch with her father. He nodded and she put in the call. Mr. Drew was neither in his office nor at home. According to his secretary, the lawyer was in Washington.

"If he calls here, I'll give him your message," she told Nancy.

The girls went to the dining room for lunch but did not talk about the mystery, afraid that someone might overhear them. Nancy, however, could not keep her mind off it.

"One thing seems certain," she said to herself. "Since Mr. Atkin has access to Mr. Basswood's office, he must know what's going on and is in league with his employer."

She was determined to do more sleuthing in the shop. When Nancy arrived there, she asked Mr. Basswood how his assistant was.

He answered nonchalantly, "Oh, he'll be all right. Atkin gets these attacks once in a while. Doesn't watch his health."

At that moment a customer arrived and Nancy asked if she could help him. This was the beginning of a very busy afternoon for her. Mr. Basswood did not wait on anyone, so Nancy had no chance to do any investigating in the shop. At four o'clock sharp he told her to go and locked the door behind her.

As she walked toward the taxi stand, the young detective said to herself, "If I had this job as my real livelihood, I'd certainly ask for higher wages. Mr. Basswood is a selfish old meany. In the short time I've been here, I've brought him over a thousand dollars in sales."

Nancy was cheered, however, by the one possible clue she had discovered—the mysterious *M De K* notation.

A visitor was waiting for her at the yacht club. A pleasant, serious-faced man of about forty said he was Sylvester Holden and had come to examine the statue on the front lawn.

In a low tone he said, "Your father sent me."

Nancy nodded. Mr. Ayer, Bess, and George followed Nancy and Mr. Holden outdoors. The sculptor carried a small bag of tools.

"This is a fine piece," he remarked as they approached the statue. "I suspect it is a reproduction, however."

He took a strong magnifying glass from his tool kit and spent several minutes going over the statue. Presently he brought out a chisel and tapped the marble.

"It doesn't ring," he said. "An original would.

This piece is made from marble dust mixed with a white casting cement. But I must say it's one of the finest reproductions I've ever seen."

"Do you think it was made in this country?" Mr. Ayer asked.

Mr. Holden said there was no way of being sure, but he suspected that it had been made in the United States. "I think this is powdered Vermont marble."

Nancy spoke up. "Can you give us any clue about how we might find out who the sculptor was?"

"That depends on whether or not the person who made the piece wanted to keep his identity a secret. Most sculptors and makers of reproductions put a mark on the base of the statue. Let's turn this lady on her side and take a look."

"Let's hope it hasn't been cemented down," Nancy remarked.

She was relieved to find this had not been done yet. The statue was tipped over and gently laid on the lawn. Everyone peered at the base.

"I see something!" Nancy exclaimed. "It's very faint, but it says *M De K!*"

CHAPTER XII

Unexpected Clue

Bess and George also stared at the initials on the base of the statue. "M De K!" they exclaimed, recalling what Nancy had told them about the notation in Mr. Basswood's office.

Turning to Mr. Holden, Nancy asked, "Do you know a sculptor with the initials M De K?"

"No, but I can look up this person in my directory of painters and sculptors. I'll do it as soon as I get back to New York and I'll let you know."

The statue was set in place again. As Mr. Holden walked back to the clubhouse with the girls and Mr. Ayer, he offered to consult various trade journals to find out who had sold the original whispering statue.

"Also who purchased it, and what the price was. But don't get your hopes up too high," he warned. "I'm inclined to think it was a secret deal and not reported because the whispering statue was stolen.

Later I'll take some measurements of this reproduction. These will be the same size as the original."

"How can that be?" Bess spoke up.

Mr. Holden explained that the rubbery material a sculptor brushes over the original work produces a skin-tight mold. "The cast which is made from the mold is therefore the same size as the original.

"And I would say that the patina of the stolen statue—meaning its surface color—would be somewhat different from that of the lady out on the lawn, even though the reproduction is an excellent one."

George asked, "Mr. Holden, could the thief have sold the original statue at such a high price he became worried and tried to ward off suspicion by having a reproduction made to try to fool people?"

"Oh yes," the sculptor replied. "I would say that the original was worth many thousands of dollars."

"Hypers!" George burst out. Then she said, "I wonder if this M De K is in league with the thief —or if he was just paid to do a job without knowing the reason."

Mr. Ayer looked at the girls and smiled. "I expect Debbie Lynbrook and her friends to find that out."

Mr. Holden proved to be a fascinating companion and related many interesting and amusing stories about his work.

"I think my worst subject was a small boy whose mother wanted a statue of her little darling. But the boy couldn't sit still for more than fifteen seconds at a time. He seemed scared to death of me every time I came near him with a tape measure. Finally I gave up and just took a lot of pictures of him."

The girls laughed and George asked, "How did it all work out? Did you make the statue?"

"Oh yes," Mr. Holden answered. "But I had to charge the mother a rather high price for all the extra time it took."

During a slight lull in the conversation, Nancy asked the sculptor if he would stop at Basswood's Art and Bookshop the following morning.

"I'd like you to look over the statues and statuettes and see if they're fairly priced."

"I'll be glad to," Mr. Holden promised. "Since I'll be going through the town on my way home, I'll drive you there."

Suddenly he began to chuckle. "It's possible Mr. Basswood may think he recognizes me from photographs he might have seen in magazines or newspapers, so I believe I'll change my name too. How about Harry Silver?"

"I'll remember," Nancy answered. "I think it's a good idea."

The next morning, when they arrived at the

shop, Nancy had a hard time keeping a straight face as she said to Mr. Basswood, "I'd like you to meet Mr. Harry Silver. He was staying at the yacht club and offered to drive me over. Mr. Silver, this is Mr. Basswood."

The two men shook hands, then the visitor was invited to sign the register. Nancy was confident Harry Silver, New York City, was a good disguise. She went on, "May I show Mr. Silver some of our fine pieces?"

"Go ahead. I'll be in my office any time you need me." Whenever the shop owner disappeared, Nancy wondered if he had some secret means of spying on her.

She showed Mr. Silver some of the fine paintings, but he shook his head and said, "How about some of the statuettes? This is an attractive one." He pointed toward a boy, wearing ragged knee trousers and a loose-sleeved, low-necked shirt. He was barefoot and carried a fishing pole over one shoulder.

As Mr. Holden picked up the statuette, Mr. Basswood suddenly reappeared and watched him sharply. The sculptor turned the piece over and looked at the base.

He whistled. "This is highly priced," he remarked, and set the statuette down. "Too much money for me."

Some of Nancy's suspicions had been confirmed! She gave no sign of her elation.

"Mr. Silver," she said, "perhaps you would be interested in a smaller piece." She led him to the statuette of a man seated cross-legged and whittling a piece of wood.

"That is interesting," he commented. Once more he turned the statuette over and looked at the sales sticker. Then he sighed. "I'm afraid there isn't anything here within my price range."

Mr. Basswood's eyes flashed. "Sculptors don't give away their work," he snapped.

"And these are originals?" Mr. Silver asked.

"Of course."

The caller said he guessed he would have to go somewhere else and buy a copy. Nancy noted that the sculptor avoided the word reproduction. She also wondered if the pieces were not originals. She hoped for an opportunity to ask Mr. Silver.

When the sculptor said he must leave, because he had a long drive back to New York City, she followed him to the door. Mr. Basswood went along, so there was no chance for her to speak privately to Mr. Holden. Disappointed, she said good-by and closed the door.

Turning to Mr. Basswood, she asked, "How is Mr. Atkin?"

"Coming along. It was certainly mighty inconsiderate of him to pick a time like this to get sick. You know yourself how rushed we've been here."

Nancy pretended to look hurt. "I'm doing the best I can, Mr. Basswood."

"Yes, yes, I know," he said. "But we've got to keep this place cleaner. Go get a dustcloth and wipe off the books."

Before Nancy went for it, she remarked, "When Mr. Silver turned over the statuette, I noticed the initials M De K on the base. What do they stand for?"

Was it her imagination, or did Mr. Basswood show a sudden bit of alarm?

His fright was gone in a moment and he replied, "I really don't know. I bought those pieces at an auction and never did inquire who the sculptor was." He turned toward the rare book section and Nancy went to the back room for the dustcloth.

Unlike other mornings, half an hour went by and not a customer had come in. Nancy said to her employer, "Since I've finished the dusting and there isn't any special work to do in the shop, is there anything I can help you with in the office?"

Mr. Basswood's face took on a dark look. "You stay out of my office!" he almost shouted at her. "Get another cloth and dust off the paintings."

She was back in a few seconds—apparently before Mr. Basswood expected her. She had seen him take a book from a shelf and upon hearing her footsteps had tucked it under his coat. She was puzzled. Why didn't he want her to know he had it?

"I wonder what the book is," she thought.

As soon as she had dusted the paintings, Nancy went over to the bookshelves. Because of her special interest in the books, she had memorized the titles of all the volumes. In a few moments she realized that Mr. Basswood had taken one on modern painters and sculptors. Did he think M De K was mentioned in it and did not want her to find out?

As she stood in the book section mulling over this, suddenly the whole building began to shake. Statuettes, paintings, and books flew through the air.

"It must be an earthquake!" Nancy thought, trying to keep her balance.

The next instant an enormous book was dislodged from an upper shelf and fell directly toward her head!

CHAPTER XIII

Living Pictures

NANCY saw the heavy volume falling and jumped aside. The big book crashed to the floor inches from her feet. The violent shaking of the earth ceased abruptly.

Mr. Basswood had rushed from his office and into the street. Nancy, too, hurried toward the doorway. She could see people running and hear shouts of "What happened?" "Was it an earthquake?"

Noticing that Mr. Basswood's office door was open, Nancy ran inside and turned on the radio to a local station. She was just in time to hear, "We interrupt this broadcast to give you a report on the earth tremor in Waterford.

"It was not an earthquake. There was a gas-main break underground with a resultant explosion. All danger is over but everyone is asked to be sure gas burners are turned off. We will broadcast a further report as soon as it is received."

The young detective made a quick survey of the office. Half buried under a pile of papers that had shifted on Mr. Basswood's desk was the volume he had removed from the bookshelf.

Hearing Mr. Basswood's footsteps, Nancy tucked the volume under her arm and scooted back into the main room. Quickly she hid the book behind some others, and began picking up the volumes that had fallen to the floor.

Mr. Basswood walked toward her, saying, "This is terrible, terrible! What a loss!"

"You're insured, of course?" Nancy asked him. He did not reply and Nancy could not decide whether it was because he did not want to, or because he was not paying attention to her question. He went outdoors.

All around the shop paintings lay upside down on the floor and nearly every art object in the place had fallen over. Nancy noticed a statuette that had slipped from a pedestal to the floor and cracked wide open. It was tagged as an original marble piece and highly priced. Nancy was amazed to see that it had an inner metal armature to support the arms and legs. The piece was not solid marble but a reproduction made of white cement and marble dust!

"And not worth what Mr. Basswood was asking for it," she thought.

On a hunch Nancy picked up the base of the statue. She was not surprised to see M De K faintly carved into it.

"I must find out who that person is," Nancy said to herself as she began to pick up the scattered pieces.

Half an hour later Mr. Basswood came back. "I'm going to close the shop for the day. There's too much of a mess in the place for customers to shop. You go on home, Miss Lynbrook. I'll send for you when I want you back."

"But I don't like to leave you with all the cleaning up to do," Nancy remarked. "I'll stay and help."

Instead of being grateful, the shop owner looked at his employee angrily. "I said go and I mean go." He pointed toward the door.

Nancy shrugged. "All right, if you say so."

As she went to get her coat from the back room, Mr. Basswood returned to his office. In the rear room of the shop, Nancy found things topsy-turvy. To her amazement a large highboy had slid out of place, revealing a hidden door.

"I wonder what's behind the door," Nancy thought. "And how much damage has been done."

She opened the door and gazed into a dim room with a small skylight. Nancy could vaguely see small pieces of statuary on the floor, sculpting tools which apparently had fallen from a workbench, and several large portrait frames. These stood along one wall on which hung an enormous canvas cloth. Miraculously the frames had not toppled over.

"I must investigate this room further," Nancy thought.

She closed the door, put on her coat, and walked toward the front entrance. Mr. Basswood was standing there. He held the door open, impatient for her to leave. Hurrying toward the shop were Bess and George. The cousins looked excited.

"You all right?" they asked Nancy. And Bess added, "Wasn't the quake a fright?" The two girls stepped into the hallway of the shop.

"Oh, Mr. Basswood, you're to go to the hospital immediately," George told him.

"What!" he exclaimed.

Bess said the two girls had taken an injured woman to the hospital. "The patients there were pretty frightened. We went up to see Mr. Atkin. He kept saying he had to talk to you at once, and that somebody must go get you immediately."

A look of alarm came over Mr. Basswood's face. Then he regained his composure. "You're sure of this?" he asked.

Both Bess and George nodded. Bess said, "We told him we were coming over to your shop and would tell you."

Mr. Basswood looked skeptical. Did he suspect

some trick? He asked, "If Atkin wanted me in such a hurry, why didn't he telephone?"

"The nurse at the desk said she'd tried but your phone didn't answer," George said.

"It didn't ring," the shop owner said. "Did it, Miss Lynbrook?"

"No. I'll go try it now and see if it's out of order."

"You stay out of my office!" Mr. Basswood said firmly.

Nancy was eager to do some real sleuthing. If she could get Mr. Basswood to go to the hospital and leave her there, she would have an opportunity to look around for clues. To her relief Mr. Basswood turned, went back to his office, and closed the door.

Quickly Nancy whispered to the girls, "Don't go! Hide some place."

George took the cue. In a loud voice she said, "Come on, Debbie! Hurry! What say we go have some fun?"

Nancy grinned gratefully, then closed the front door with a bang. Quickly she tiptoed to the rear room and slipped behind the highboy. Bess and George had already hidden themselves in the large room.

Seconds later they heard the shop owner lock his office door from the outside. He walked through the hall and let himself out the front door. When Bess and George felt sure he was not going to return, they hurried to the back room.

"What do you want us to do?" George asked Nancy.

"Follow me and I'll show you."

Bess grabbed the other two girls. "This is awfully scary. Suppose we're caught!"

"We'll have to take that chance," Nancy told her. "I found a hidden room. There are lots of things in it."

She opened the door and tried to find a light switch on the wall but could not locate one. Figuring there might be a hanging light over the workbench, she started toward it.

"Shouldn't we shut the door?" Bess queried.

"Yes," Nancy replied.

By this time the girls' eyes had become accustomed to the small amount of light which filtered through the dusty skylight. Bess and George were intrigued by the huge picture frames. They were old and covered with gold leaf.

Nancy noticed a stack of books, tied up, that stood on the floor. "I wonder if they're part of Mrs. Merriam's collection," she thought. "I'll look."

She walked over to the pile and her suspicions were confirmed. A card had been tucked under the cord. There was one word on it—Merriam.

Before the girls had a chance to examine the

books, they heard heavy footsteps outside the door. Nancy knew they were not Mr. Basswood's. Was there a burglar in the shop? And what should she do?

Instantly the young detective made a decision. Grabbing Bess and George by their arms, she pointed toward the empty portrait frames.

"Pose!" Nancy whispered.

The three girls stepped through the frames against the canvas. Each one kneeled and took a different pose. They assumed profile positions so they could not be identified easily if the intruder should happen to know them.

"This is fearful," Bess thought nervously, but she held very still. George and Nancy held rigid poses.

The door opened and a muscular man clomped into the room. Nancy almost forgot to hold her pose. He was the man who had forced his way into the Drew house by their front door and attacked her father!

"I must capture him!" she told herself but wondered how to do so.

The man began looking around and mumbling to himself. At first the girls could not distinguish any words but presently he talked louder.

"The money's got to be here somewhere!" he said. "He owes it to Marco and me. We got a right to take it!"

The girls held rigid poses as the intruder entered the room

In his search the newcomer suddenly lurched into Bess's frame. It fell over, striking Bess who also went down. Instantly the intruder realized that the person in the frame was alive!

"Oh!" cried Bess.

The man gave a deep grunt, then yanked Bess up from the floor. At the same instant Nancy and George leaped from their frames!

CHAPTER XIV

Suspicious Caller

THE intruder was taken completely by surprise. It was easy for the three girls to hold him. As he became obstreperous, George used a judo trick which buckled the man's knees and he fell.

"Let me go!" he shouted.

"Hold him!" Nancy said. "I'll get the police!" She was sure George with Bess's help could manage the man until officers arrived.

In her excitement Nancy forgot to disguise her voice and wondered if the intruder might have recognized it.

"I hope not."

She raced from the shop to a corner pay telephone a block away and called the police. Nancy explained the situation to Captain Turner. He promised to send a squad car at once.

As she hung up, a disturbing thought occurred to Nancy. Although the police captain could be relied upon to keep her real identity a secret, Debbie Lynbrook's part in the incident was bound to come out.

"Mr. Basswood will know I was investigating the place. He's so suspicious of me already he'll probably discharge me."

As Nancy ran back to the art shop, she hoped that Bess and George had been able to hold the man. A moment later she saw the shop door burst open. The girls' captive was running away! Nancy was too far away to stop him, but in a moment Bess and George dashed from the building.

By this time the man had sped across the street and jumped into a car with its motor running. A companion who sat at the wheel immediately took off.

Nancy cried out, "Stop! Stop!" and ran into the street.

Instantly the driver swerved in her direction as if he intended to run her down. She jumped back to the sidewalk just in time.

"What luck!" she thought. "I wonder what happened."

By this time Bess and George had come up to her. Shamefaced, they said that despite George's judo skill, they had been unable to hold the man.

"He has muscles like steel," George remarked. "Sorry, Nancy."

Bess spoke up. "We did our best. Who do you think the man was—a burglar?"

Nancy explained that he was the man who had escaped through the front entrance of the Drew home the night Mrs. Merriam was there.

"Since he didn't break into the art shop, he must have a key to it," said George. "This is proof that he's in league with Mr. Basswood."

"Yes," Nancy replied. "I've been sure of that ever since he broke into our house and attacked Dad. Well, girls," she added, "let's hope the police catch him. And don't feel too bad about 'losing your man.' We got a valuable clue."

"We did?" Bess asked blankly.

Nancy pointed out that the intruder had murmured the name Marco. She at once thought of M De K. "The person could be Marco De K?" the young detective said excitedly. "And if he's tied in with the mystery of the whispering statue, Marco may know where it is. We must try to find him."

"Apparently," George added, "Mr. Basswood owes Marco and this man a large sum of money."

"Do you suppose," Bess suggested, "that Mr. Basswood keeps a lot of money in the shop? For instance, in that hidden room?"

"Very likely," Nancy replied. A moment later she added in dismay, "We've locked ourselves out! And that book on painters and sculptors is inside! Now I can't check to see if M De K or a Marco De K is mentioned in it!"

"Cheer up!" Bess urged. "Here come the police. Maybe they can open the door."

Two officers arrived in a car and were given the details of what had happened and also the license number of the car in which the intruder had escaped.

"I'm Debbie Lynbrook and I work at the shop," Nancy added.

George spoke up. "That man didn't get anything. By the way, he forced his way into the Drew home in River Heights. The police are still looking for him."

The girls gave a minute description of the man, then Nancy asked if the officers had any way of getting into the art shop. They shook their heads.

Before the officers stepped into their car, Nancy said, "We're staying at the yacht club. If you pick up this man, will you please call Mr. Ayer and tell him. He can pass the message on to us." The men promised to do so and left.

As the girls started for the taxi stand, Bess stopped abruptly. "Wait a minute!" she said. "I just had a horrible thought! Suppose that thug tells Mr. Basswood he saw us in the shop?"

Nancy frowned. "He may, but more likely he'll be afraid to tell because Mr. Basswood would know he was poking around the shop."

When the girls arrived at the yacht club, it was near lunchtime and Bess declared she was starving. "I could go for a great big steak and French fries and a chocolate fudge sundae," she said.

George looked at her cousin sternly. "Eat all

the steak you want but no French fries or sundaes. How about substituting a big bowl of spinach and a grapefruit?" Her cousin did not reply. She merely made a face at George.

Everyone was talking about the gas-main explosion and what damage it had done. They asked Debbie Lynbrook about the art shop and were sorry to hear that some statuary and paintings had been ruined.

Nancy suddenly thought of the statue on the front lawn of the yacht club. "Is it all right?" she asked the people at the next table.

"Yes," a woman replied. "The earth tremor wasn't felt that badly up here."

Mr. Basswood did not telephone Nancy to come back so the three girls put on beach clothes and wandered down to the dock. Dick was there.

"Hi!" he said. "You're just the people I was going to contact. Debbie and George, how about you and Ned and Burt entering the races this weekend?"

"It would be fun," said George, "but we don't know whether or not the boys are coming down."

Nancy remarked. "If we enter, we'll certainly need a little practice."

Dick suggested that the girls go out now. Bess said she would stay ashore this time. She giggled. "I don't want to get dumped into the water again."

Nancy and George exchanged smiles. They

knew that Bess preferred staying on land and talking to Dick, who was certainly a most attractive companion. They rowed out to *Top Job* and climbed in. Nancy set the sails while George handled the tiller. There was a stiff offshore breeze and Nancy began tacking.

For a while the girls were the only sailors on the bay. Then a craft larger than theirs headed toward them at racing speed. Nancy and George thought nothing about it until suddenly they realized that the skipper was not going to give them the right of way.

"Nancy, there's no identification on his boat and look at him!" George cried out.

"He's wearing a stocking mask!" Nancy exclaimed.

It was evident the stranger not only did not want to be recognized, but that his plan was to upset *Top Job* and injure the girls.

"Hard alee!" yelled Nancy and swung the boom. She avoided the other boat by inches. Nancy still ran with the wind toward the clubhouse dock. Twice her pursuer tacked across her bow but each time she zigzagged out of his way and got back on course. Finally he gave up and headed toward the ocean.

George heaved a sigh. "What do you make of that?"

Nancy admitted she was puzzled. "That skipper may be someone we've seen. I'm sure he's part of the gang that would like to see us quit work on one or both of our cases."

When the girls reached shore they told Bess and Dick what had happened. Dick said he would report the incident to the police at once. "That guy out there is a menace."

"Agreed," George replied.

Bess said that Dick had offered his car to the girls for the rest of the afternoon.

"Terrific," said George.

Nancy smiled. "Thanks a lot, Dick. That's great."

The girls went to their bedroom to change into street clothes. As they opened the door, the telephone was ringing. Nancy scooped it up.

"Debbie Lynbrook?" a male voice asked.

"Yes."

"Hello. This is Sylvester Holden. I have some interesting information for you. There is a man named Marco De Keer who makes very fine reproductions. He lives in Readville, which is about twenty-five miles from Waterford. If you can get over there, I suggest you pay him a visit."

"We'll certainly do that," Nancy said, "and thank you very much, Mr. Harry Silver." She and Mr. Holden laughed over his pseudonym.

When Nancy told her chums the news, George was excited and eager to meet Marco De Keer.

Bess said she was a little scared to do so if he were a pal of Basswood's. "And speaking of pals, I wonder if the police have caught that man who got away from George and me."

"I'll find out," said Nancy and dialed police headquarters.

Captain Turner said he had no news to give her. "We think the man has left this area, but there is still an alarm out for his arrest."

The three girls finally got started for Readville. When Nancy drove into Waterford, she did not take the highway but began weaving through various streets.

"What's going on?" George asked. "Are you giving us a sightseeing trip of this town?"

Nancy explained that she was trying to elude any car which might be following her. "At the moment we know that at least three people don't trust us—Mr. Basswood, Mr. Atkin, and the man who attacked my father and came into the art shop."

George nodded. "And don't forget the guy who tried to capsize us on the bay and those kidnappers."

After Nancy was sure no one was on her trail, she drove to the highway and headed the car toward Readville. The trip was made quickly. She learned that Marco De Keer's studio and workshop were in an old barn on the outskirts of town.

The front yard was filled with terra-cotta statues which stood amid high grass. Here and there a rosebush reared its head above an overgrown flower bed, and a few hollyhocks towered above the weeds.

Nancy did not pull into the driveway but parked across the road. She chuckled. "For a quick getaway if necessary."

The large double doors of the barn were wide open. The girls walked in. On display were statues of many sizes, made of various materials. There were a few marble pieces and the girls wondered if these were originals from which Marco De Keer was making reproductions. The rest of the barn was cluttered and untidy.

Bess and George decided to go outside and look at the sculptures in the yard. "Maybe we can pick up a clue for you, Nancy," George said.

The young detective walked through the barn and found a man in a rear room just putting on a white smock. As Nancy said, "Good afternoon," he turned around.

"Oh. How do you do?" he said. "You startled me. Why didn't you ring the bell?"

"I'm sorry," Nancy answered. "I didn't see one. Are you Marco De Keer?"

"Yes. Who sent you here?"

As Nancy was trying to make up her mind how to answer his question, she appraised the man intently. He was middle-aged and had a swarthy complexion. His dark hair was long and he wore a full beard. De Keer's outstanding feature were his black eyes which glistened intensely.

"He may be talented," Nancy thought, "but I'll bet he's cruel and scheming."

Aloud she said, "I wasn't exactly sent here. Your name was given to me by a man in New York who knows a lot about statuary. He suggested that I might find a statuette I like." Nancy gave the man a naïve smile. "I can't afford an original marble."

"I see," Mr. De Keer replied. "Well, look around, and if you see anything you like, let me know. But I warn you, my prices are high."

Nancy made no comment. She went back to the main part of the barn and started looking around. Presently she picked up the statuette of a monkey and turned it over. On the base were the telltale initials M De K.

Meanwhile Bess and George had been walking around outside. Bess happened to glance down the road and saw an approaching car. The next instant she grabbed her cousin's arm.

"Here comes Mr. Basswood!" she cried. "We must warn Nancy!"

CHAPTER XV

An Abrupt Departure

BESS was in a panic. "If we run inside, Mr. Basswood will see us!"

"And if we don't," George replied, "Nancy will be trapped!"

Bess added, "If we don't show ourselves but call out Debbie or Nancy, he'll be sure to hear it."

By this time Basswood had pulled into the driveway alongside the barn and parked in the rear. Nancy, having heard the automobile, appeared in the big doorway. Bess and George signaled to her frantically to come outside.

The young detective hurried to her friends and asked, "What's up?"

Quickly George explained and Bess said, "We'd better get away from here as soon as possible!"

"And lose the chance of obtaining a valuable bit of evidence?" Nancy asked. She turned to Bess. "Here are the car keys. Suppose you drive it around the bend out of sight. Then Mr. De Keer will think we've left."

As Bess scooted off, Nancy and George hid behind large terra-cotta statues and waited to see what would happen. In a moment the two men came from the rear into the large showroom.

"It was a catastrophe!" Mr. Basswood was storming. "They said it was a gas-main explosion. Felt like an earthquake. I lost a lot of things and need some more statuettes." Suddenly his mood changed and he laughed. "I want real pieces, of course."

Marco De Keer laughed uproariously. "You've come to the right place, my friend. My originals are so original nobody knows the difference!"

George whispered to Nancy, "The cheat! Let's go in there and confront the two of them with the truth."

Nancy restrained George. "I'm afraid we'd come out the losers."

Just then Mr. De Keer said, "A girl walked in here a little while ago looking for an inexpensive reproduction. Said somebody in New York City had told her about me."

Mr. Basswood looked apprehensive. "What did she look like?"

Marco De Keer described Debbie Lynbrook exactly.

"Where is she now?" Mr. Basswood asked. alarm showing in his voice.

"I suppose she drove off. Anyway, her car is gone."

Basswood burst out, "I'm sure that's the girl who works for me. Her name is Debbie Lynbrook. I don't entirely trust her—not that she would steal anything, but she's kind of nosy. I'd fire her, only she's an excellent saleswoman. As you know, Atkin is in the hospital. He'll be coming out pretty soon, though, and then I think I'll get rid of the girl."

Nancy chuckled inwardly. Basswood did not call her Nancy Drew! He might think Debbie Lynbrook was a bit nosy, but at least he did not suspect that his employee was Nancy Drew, the young detective!

George called softly, "Are you ready to leave? Those men may come outside at any moment."

Nancy nodded. She most certainly did not want to be caught and this was a good time to vanish. Dodging among statues, the two girls reached the roadway and hurried to where they were to meet Bess.

"Thank goodness you're here," she said. "I was imagining all sorts of things about your becoming prisoners of those two men. What did you find out?"

"A good bit," Nancy replied, "but I want to learn more. I noticed a restaurant in that house next to the barn. Why don't we have an early dinner there and watch the barn from the window?"

"Food. Super!" Bess said. "I vote for that."

She drove the car to the restaurant, turned into its driveway, and parked in the rear. There was a side entrance so the three friends entered through this door.

The first floor of the farmhouse had been converted into a charming, old-fashioned dining room. A pleasant-faced woman, who reminded Nancy of Hannah Gruen, showed them to a table next to a window. It overlooked a low hedge between the two properties.

"We have no printed menus," the restaurant owner said. "Tonight we have homemade vegetable soup, baked ham or pot roast, sweet potatoes, and some of my home-canned peaches with chocolate cake for dessert. Maybe you noticed my orchards. The peaches grew right here."

Bess sighed. "It must be heavenly living on a farm and raising all your own produce. Do you have chickens and cows and everything?"

The woman, who said her name was Mrs. Ziegler, beamed. "Yes, everything."

Nancy asked where she kept the livestock. "I see the barn near you is a sculptor's studio."

Mrs. Ziegler said that the barn had not belonged to her farm. "We keep our horses and cows and chickens across the road."

Bess smiled at her and said, "Your baked-ham dinner sounds marvelous. I'll have it. And you might add a glass of milk from one of your cows."

Nancy and George decided to have the same dinner as Bess. When the soup was served, the three girls were looking out the window. Willis Basswood and Marco De Keer were driving off together in the art dealer's car.

"I wonder if they've left for the day," Bess spoke up.

Mrs. Ziegler said, "I guess so. The sculptor doesn't stay around very long." She smiled. "He doesn't keep farmers' hours!"

George asked the woman what kind of a sculptor Mr. De Keer was. "Famous?"

Mrs. Ziegler shrugged. "Statuary isn't one of my interests, so I've never paid attention to the man. He's rather a man of mystery. Hardly anyone comes there except a trucker. I guess he brings supplies and carries away statues."

Mrs. Ziegler walked off and did not return until the girls had finished the vegetable soup. In the meantime they discussed the man next door.

"So he's a person of mystery who makes ugly statues!" George said.

"We already know that," Bess remarked. "Nancy, how do you plan to find out more about this suspect?"

The young detective's eyes sparkled. "As soon as we finish eating, I'm going back to Mr. De Keer's place and do more investigating."

"But surely," George said, "he must have locked the barn."

"Oh, I wasn't going to trespass," Nancy told her. "We may find some clues on the grounds around the barn."

Half an hour later the girls paid their checks and then strolled over to the Marco De Keer place. Most of the statues were made of terra cotta and were grotesque. Among them was a two-headed monster and a tall skinny figure with an elongated head that rose to a peak and had slanted eyes and an upturned mouth.

"These would give me a nightmare," Bess remarked.

"Let's try tipping this one over to see if it has M De K on the bottom," Nancy suggested.

The statue, though large, was not heavy and the girls laid the figure on its side easily. Stuck to the bottom of it was part of a torn letter.

"How did this get here?" Bess asked.

"My guess is," said Nancy, "that pieces of a letter were thrown away but this scrap must have missed the basket or been blown by the wind and plastered itself to the bottom of the statues."

"What does it say?" George asked, walking around Nancy to read it.

"Another puzzle," said Bess. "What does it mean?"

The words on the jagged piece of paper were:

> *time to move*
> *competitors are be-*
> *picious. Stop work*
> *ble reproductions.*
> *phone from Pit*
> *soon as I look*
> *whispering statue*

Quickly Nancy took a notebook from her purse and copied the words in case she lost the original paper.

"What a marvelous clue!" she exclaimed.

CHAPTER XVI

Unwelcome Command

"Your clue is wonderful," said Bess, "but how can you use it? The words in that torn letter don't make any sense to me."

George said, "Why don't we drive back to the yacht club? You can study it there, Nancy."

The young detective did not want to leave yet. "Let's search for the rest of the letter," she said.

The girls turned over all the pieces of statuary but found nothing. The hedge and every bit of the ground around the barn were scrutinized carefully. No other clues were found.

Finally Nancy agreed to leave. The girls climbed into Dick's car and started for Waterford.

After they had been driving about fifteen minutes, George said, "Nancy, have you figured out anything about the torn note?"

"Yes, I have one hunch. Bess, please look in the

glove compartment and see if there's a map of this area."

As Bess was rummaging through a stack of maps, she asked, "What's on your mind?"

Nancy said she believed the Pit in the note stood for a town. "And I have a hunch it's one not far from here."

"How did you arrive at that conclusion?" George asked.

"First of all, I'm sure I recognized the handwriting on that note. It is definitely Willis Basswood's."

"Really?" Bess said in amazement. "Then he knows about the whispering statue and where it is?"

"Exactly," Nancy replied. "He probably sold it secretly to someone who doesn't live far away, so it wouldn't be seen on the road. I believe that person is in Pit something. Bess, did you find the map?"

A local map was on the bottom of the pile. Bess pulled out the folded sheet and opened it. "Pit— Pit—Pit— Oh, here's one. Pittville. Nancy, you're a genius!"

"Don't praise me yet. I may be on the wrong track. Is there another town beginning with Pit?"

Bess's forefinger was moving over the map. Presently she cried out, "Here's a town with the name Pitman!"

"Any more Pits?" George asked. "Don't find one that says Pitfall."

Nancy and Bess smiled and Bess remarked, "That's pretty corny."

Nancy was glad that no more towns beginning P-i-t were in the vicinity. "Tomorrow we'll go to Pittville and then to Pitman."

"In what?" Bess asked. Then she added hopefully, "Maybe Dick will lend us his car again. He's a great guy."

George remarked, "If Mr. Basswood stole the statue, it probably was taken directly to Marco De Keer's barn. After the reproduction was finished, their trucker friend delivered the original to the purchaser and brought the reproduction to the yacht club."

Bess giggled. "The mystery is practically solved. All you have to find out is when and where and who did what and why?"

When the girls returned to their room at the yacht club the telephone was ringing. The caller was Mr. Drew. He asked Nancy how she was progressing on the case.

"I hate to brag," Nancy replied, "but we really have some fabulous clues." She related everything that she and her friends had learned since her last report.

Mr. Drew was elated but admitted he was worried about Nancy's safety. "Don't work for Mr.

Basswood unless Bess and George come and check on you every so often."

"All right, Dad. Anyway, I don't think I'll be there much longer. Mr. Basswood says Mr. Atkin is leaving the hospital very soon and will be back to work. By the way, Dad, where are you calling from?"

"Washington, D. C. I'm still working on my case here." He chuckled. "You'll probably get home before I do and solve this whole mystery yourself."

"I hope you're right," Nancy said, laughing. "And I'm glad that so far no one has seen through my disguise."

Mr. Drew said good-by and Nancy turned to talk to Bess and George. They had changed their clothes and were ready to go downstairs.

"I'll meet you as soon as I take off these dusty clothes and put on fresh ones. Oh, I guess my wig needs a good brushing too."

Fifteen minutes later she joined Bess and George in the lobby of the club. They were talking with Dick.

"We may borrow Dick's car tomorrow," Bess announced.

Dick spoke up. "I won't need it. If I have to go to town, I'll use the truck."

"I certainly appreciate the offer, Dick," said Nancy. She grinned at him. "You're always coming to our rescue. We ought to take time out to do something for you."

"Debbie Lynbrook, you've just said exactly the right thing. You can do something for me right now."

"What's that?" Nancy asked.

Dick explained that he had reserved one of the Ping-pong tables in the recreation room, hoping the girls would join him in a doubles match.

George beamed. "That's a groovy way of paying a debt."

The four young people went downstairs. After a toss of paddles, the partners turned out to be Dick and George against Nancy and Bess. At the end of two games the score stood one to one. Dick complimented all the girls on their playing.

"You're champs," he said.

Bess called to him, "You're terrific yourself, but Debbie and I are going to win this game."

There were long volleys and some breath-taking net shots. But in the end Nancy and Bess won the game.

"We told you so!" Bess gloated.

But the next game went to Dick and George. After half an hour of hard, fast playing the score stood even, but in the final game Dick and George scored the twenty-first point and were declared the victors.

Bess flopped into a chair. "I'm absolutely pooped," she said.

Dick looked at her. "Would a sundae with fudge sauce revive you? I hear that's one of your favorite dishes."

"It sure would," Bess replied. "It's a beautiful idea. Let's go!"

The four went into the club's snack shop. Over the loudspeaker came the announcement, "Miss Debbie Lynbrook is wanted on the phone."

Nancy excused herself and went to a telephone on the wall of the shop.

"This is Mr. Basswood," the caller said. "Miss Lynbrook, I want you here at nine o'clock tomorrow morning."

Nancy hesitated. If she worked all day, she would not be able to drive to Pittville and Pitman to continue her sleuthing. And she was determined not to give that up!

"Did you hear me?" Mr. Basswood asked impatiently.

"Yes," Nancy replied. "I'll be there at nine, but I'll have to leave at two-thirty."

Mr. Basswood's voice was icy as he said, "All right, but I'll expect you to forgo your lunch hour. Good-by."

As Nancy returned to her friends, she frowned a little and said to herself, "What an old grouch he is!"

A little later Dick said he must leave. The girls continued to talk. Nancy told the cousins about her phone call from Mr. Basswood. "But I'll be able to leave at two-thirty. Suppose we drive directly to Pittville then."

"It's only about twenty miles from here," Bess said.

When the girls were ready to go upstairs, Nancy said, "You don't mind if I stay down here a little while? I'd like to stroll outside and do some thinking."

"We don't mind," Bess assured her. "But don't be late. Mr. Basswood would not like it if his star salesman came to work hollow-eyed and weary."

As Nancy walked toward the bay side of the club, she found herself heading toward the statue. A stiff breeze was blowing and she was forced to hold onto her wig. As she neared the marble figure, Nancy suddenly stopped.

"The statue is whispering!" she told herself.

No one was around. Deep, garbled words seemed to be issuing from the statue's mouth.

"There must be a reasonable explanation for this," Nancy thought. "But it's weird and eerie just the same."

She moved back a little distance to gaze at the marble lady. At the same instant two dark shadows crossed that of the statue.

A man's harsh voice whispered, "Her friends are here, but where's Nancy Drew?"

Another hard voice replied, "She must be around here. We'll find her!"

Nancy's heart was thumping. She was well hidden in the shadow of the yacht club. Should she stay there or run into the clubhouse?

"That might be a giveaway," she decided, and stayed where she was.

Just then the first voice said, "Here comes somebody! We'd better scram!"

The shadowy figures disappeared and Nancy could hear running footsteps. Although she had not been able to identify the men, the young sleuth knew from their voices that they were two of the thugs who had tried to kidnap her and Bess and George at the deserted mansion on the beach. She wondered if her enemies had discovered she was wearing a disguise.

Relieved that the men had not seen her, Nancy walked quickly back to the clubhouse. She went to her room at once and told George and Bess what had happened.

"Thank goodness you're safe," said Bess. "From now on we're never going to leave you alone. And you say the statue whispered? It's uncanny."

"What did it say?" George asked.

"The lady only mumbled," Nancy replied. "I couldn't figure out anything."

The following morning the three girls went to the art shop together. It had been cleaned and set in order. While Nancy waited on customers, Bess and George roamed through the large display room. Once the owner came from his office and glared at them, but said nothing.

Just before twelve o'clock Nancy made a big sale. She carried the painting to Mr. Basswood's office and knocked.

The door swung open. Mr. Basswood did not take the painting as he usually did. Instead, he yanked Nancy inside and shoved her into a chair. He locked the door.

Angrily he said, "Stay there, young lady! Now tell me, what were you doing at Mr. De Keer's studio and why did you run off?"

CHAPTER XVII

Captured

STARTLED by Mr. Basswood's question that she tell him why she had gone to Mr. De Keer's, Nancy did not reply at once.

"I want an answer!" the shop owner demanded.

Nancy was trying to look unconcerned. She smiled at her employer.

"Someone in New York gave me his name," she said. "I thought I might save you some trouble and see if he had any pieces you could sell. He's very talented."

Mr. Basswood looked up at the ceiling, then at the floor as if trying to make up his mind whether or not she was telling the truth.

"Is that all there is to it?" he asked. "I also want to know why you left his studio in such a hurry."

Again Nancy smiled. "I saw a customer drive up, so my friends and I went next door to have dinner. We walked back to the barn later but the place was locked."

The art dealer stared at her but she gave no evidence of nervousness or concern.

The conversation was interrupted by loud banging on the office door. Nancy got up and went to open it. Bess was standing there.

"Debbie," she said, "your customer is becoming impatient waiting for her package.

Nancy looked at Mr. Basswood. His expression indicated anger and frustration. After a long pause, he said:

"Okay, I'll bring the package and the change myself. Debbie, you go back to the big room. And hereafter, I want you to mind your own business!"

Bess winked at Nancy and the two girls walked through the hall into the main room of the shop.

In a low voice Bess said, "George and I are getting tired of hanging around here and dodging behind objects to avoid Mr. Basswood."

"I'm sorry," Nancy replied. "Try to hang on a little longer. Okay?"

A few moments later Mr. Basswood came into the room with the painting wrapped carefully and the change for the customer.

Nancy was thinking, "Maybe Mr. Basswood will go off to have lunch. Then I can do some more sleuthing around here."

After the customer had left, Nancy reminded Mr. Basswood of the arrangement he had agreed to. The man's face turned red with anger and he shouted, "You can't leave early! I need you here!"

"But you promised—"

"In business," the shop owner said, "you have to put your personal affairs aside if you expect to be successful."

Nancy did not comment. She turned toward the girls and asked, "Would one of you go and buy a sandwich and bring it back to me?"

Apparently Mr. Basswood did not approve. But he must have felt that Nancy was miffed over his scolding because he gave her a half-hearted apology.

"I suppose you must eat," he said. "But I don't want any food brought in here. Run across the street to the sandwich shop. The reason I need you here this afternoon is because I planned to go shopping for more merchandise. Please stay."

George turned her back so the man could not see the broad grin that spread over her face. Mr. Basswood was actually playing right into Nancy's hands!

"I won't be returning after lunch," he told his young employee. He pulled a key from a pocket and handed it to Nancy, saying, "This is for the front door. You'll need it to let yourself in when you come back. And when you go at four, put the key on the hall table."

"Very well," Nancy replied. "And I hope I'll

make a lot of sales this afternoon. Where will I wrap the things and how do I make change for the customers?"

Mr. Basswood mulled over this question a few moments, then replied, "You'll find wrapping paper and tape in the back room. It's in a couple of the drawers in a highboy back there. I'll put some money for change in a cashbox in the top drawer."

The three girls said good-by to him and went to the sandwich shop. As soon as they sat down, Nancy said, "Will you girls please do a little sleuthing for me this afternoon."

"What do you have in mind?" Bess asked.

"I want you to follow Mr. Basswood."

"Just the two of us?" Bess asked a bit fearfully. "Who knows what that man may be up to? I don't relish being kidnapped!"

Nancy was looking out the window. The next second she jumped from her chair and rushed out the door. Bess and George looked at each other, puzzled. Then they realized why Nancy had left them so abruptly. Through a window they could see Dick walking along the street!

The young detective ran up to him and said, "You're just the person I was hoping to see! We need some help!"

"What's up?" he asked.

Quickly Nancy told him that Mr. Basswood had

left the shop for a while. "I asked George and Bess to follow him when he drives off in his car. But Bess is nervous about it."

Before Nancy could ask if he knew of a man who could join them, Dick said, "I'll be glad to go along. A friend of mine is holding down my job this afternoon."

Nancy smiled. "Great! I have a pretty good idea where Mr. Basswood's going. If I'm right, you'll be back before dinnertime."

Dick asked where his car was. Nancy told him and took the keys from her purse.

As she handed them over, he said, "I'll get the car and leave it here in front of the restaurant. From inside we can see Mr. Basswood leave and take off after him."

Dick went for the car and Nancy returned to the restaurant. She told the two girls about the arrangement and Bess said she was relieved. A few minutes later Dick joined the girls. He had not eaten lunch and ordered a roast-beef sandwich.

Although the four young people ate quickly to be ready to go at any moment, Mr. Basswood did not come out of the driveway alongside the shop for nearly an hour.

"I'll pay the check," Nancy directed. "You three scoot!"

Dick and the two girls hurried outside, jumped into Dick's car, and were soon out of sight. Nancy was eager to get back to the bookshop to do some sleuthing. She would have nearly an hour before she opened the store to customers.

Nancy paid the check and went across the street. As she was unlocking the door, a familiar voice called out, "Hi, Debbie!"

"Ned!"

The young man stepped into the shop with her, saying, "I thought we might go sailing."

"Sounds great," said Nancy, "but you forget I'm a working girl!"

"Can't you get Basswood to let you take a little time off? After all, I've come a long way to see you."

"Sorry," Nancy replied. "Mr. Basswood has just gone off for the afternoon to buy merchandise. Bess and George went with Dick to trail him in his car."

Ned's eyes lighted up. "I'd say Debbie Lynbrook has arranged a perfect setup. And I'd like to bet you intend to make a thorough search of this shop before you open the door to customers."

"You're absolutely right." Nancy laughed. "And how about helping me?"

"Anything you say."

Nancy suggested that first they go to the basement where she had seen piles of Mrs. Merriam's books through the window. The door to the cellar stairway was unlocked. She snapped on the light and started down the steps.

The next moment Nancy gasped. "There's nothing here!"

"You mean Mr. Basswood moved everything out?"

Nancy said she was sure no one else had. "I wonder why he did that. Ned, let's search the room upstairs where the picture frames are."

The highboy in the rear room had been pushed back into place but Ned moved it aside. Nancy opened the door and the couple gazed inside.

"Everything is gone from here too!" Ned exclaimed.

Nancy did not comment for several seconds, then she said, "Ned, this looks very suspicious. I think Mr. Basswood is probably planning to disappear." She glanced at her watch. It was nearly two o'clock. "I must open the shop soon," she told him. "How about your doing some more investigating in here and see if you can pick up a clue?"

"Okay."

Nancy went through the rear room toward the hall. When she reached it she stood still and stared. In the big room a burly man was scooping up objects as fast as he could and putting them into a lined, compartmented carton. Apparently he had let himself in with a key.

The man turned and she got a good look at his face. He was the one who had entered the front door of the Drew home and escaped from the art shop yesterday!

"Stop that!" Nancy yelled at him.

The intruder sprang toward her. Nancy started to run to the rear room, crying out, "Help! Ned! Help!"

The burly man grabbed hold of Nancy, pinned the girl's arms back, and began to stuff the gag into her mouth. At that instant Ned raced into the hall.

The intruder saw him and let go of Nancy. He made a dash for the front door, but Ned leaped for the man's legs and brought him down in a smashing tackle.

As he slowly rose to his feet, he said, "I got a right to be here! I was sent to take away this stuff! Let go of me!"

"Who told you to take it?" Ned demanded.

"None of your business."

Once more the intruder made a beeline for the front door, but again Ned was too quick for him. He threw the man to the floor, knocking the wind out of him. Nancy told Ned about the previous intrusion.

As he lay on the floor, Ned remarked, "You got away before, but you won't again! This time we're turning you over to the police!"

The man panicked. "No! No! Don't do that! I'll talk!"

Nancy and Ned looked at each other and

"Help! Ned! Help!" Nancy cried

waited for their prisoner to say something. He got to his knees, then stood up without a word.

Suddenly there was loud knocking on the door. Could the caller be an accomplice? Ned held onto his captive while Nancy cautiously opened the door a crack.

CHAPTER XVIII

Important Lead

To Nancy's relief she recognized the newcomer as a guest at the yacht club. Quickly she said to him, "Please get the police! We're holding a thief here!"

Terror came into the eyes of Ned's prisoner. He tried once more to get away, but Ned held him in a tight grip.

Nancy asked him, "Who gave you the key to this place?"

"Mr. Basswood. I do trucking for him." Quickly Nancy shot another question at the man. "And for Marco De Keer too?"

The prisoner stared at Nancy in disbelief. Then he said, "Sure." As if suddenly proud of his identity, the man puffed out his chest. "Trunk Rasson is strong. I can lift anything."

The young detective wanted to quiz the prisoner about having forced his way into the Drew home. But he evidently had no idea who she was and Nancy decided it would be better if he did not know. She would leave the assault charge against him to her father.

"I'm still Debbie Lynbrook," she thought, and went on with her questioning. "You say you can lift anything? Even a very heavy statue?"

"Sure. Why not?"

Nancy pursued a hunch she had. "Did you deliver a life-size marble to someone in Pitman or Pittville?"

"I sure did. And she was a beauty, too."

The man's bragging came to a sudden end. A look of fright came over his face. Apparently he realized he had talked too much. He merely shook his head when more questions were put to him.

In a few minutes the customer returned with two police officers. Trunk Rasson was taken into custody. His bravado gone, the prisoner did not attempt to escape and would say nothing.

Nancy took one of the officers aside and whispered to him, "The River Heights police are looking for this man. I suggest that you contact Chief McGinnis there."

"We'll do that," the officer replied.

Nancy went on, "Mrs. Horace Merriam in Waterford will be able to identify him."

After Rasson and his truck were taken away, Nancy and Ned discussed this latest happening.

She remarked, "I believe Rasson was supposed to remove all the worthwhile merchandise."

Ned frowned. "Nancy, I don't like the looks of this whole thing. Boy, am I glad I came when I did! When I think that you might have been a prisoner of that—"

Nancy patted her friend's arm. "You may even have saved my life!" She looked at him gratefully.

There was no chance for further conversation because customers began to arrive. Many did not intend to purchase anything—they were merely curious as to why the police had been there.

To each question Nancy would reply with a smile, "We caught a thief!"

The reactions were varied. Most of the women said, "Weren't you terrified?" The men would become angry and wish they had had a chance to overpower the burglar.

There were so many people in the shop that Ned was forced to act as salesman. He told Nancy he was enjoying himself immensely.

Shortly before closing time, a man who had purchased a rather large painting handed Nancy a hundred-dollar bill. Mr. Basswood had left a small amount of change in a drawer in the rear room. In order to save time going back and forth, Ned had been putting the cash in one of his own pockets.

He was busy at the moment so Nancy started for the highboy to see if there was enough change in the cashbox. But force of habit led her unthinkingly to Mr. Basswood's office. Then, realizing he was not there, she started away.

"Maybe the door's unlocked," she thought, "and I can find change inside."

The knob turned and the door swung inward. To her astonishment the drawers in the desk and file cabinet stood open. All were empty!

"Basswood has skipped out!" she said to herself and hurried to find Ned. She whispered her suspicions to him, then said, "Here's a hundred-dollar bill. The painting is seventy-five dollars."

Ned pulled a wad of bills from his pocket and counted out twenty-five dollars in change to the customer, then said he would wrap the painting.

"That won't be necessary," the man said. "I have a blanket in the car I can put over it." He went off.

There was no chance for Nancy to discuss with Ned what she had discovered in Mr. Basswood's office. At four o'clock all the customers left. Nancy locked the front door and the couple rushed to the office.

"You're probably right that Basswood has skipped," Ned remarked. "And I guess he really did send Rasson here to pick up the stuff. You sure fouled that little scheme of theirs!"

Nancy smiled. "What an afternoon. We have captured a suspect and taken in several hundred dollars from sales!"

"We'd better not leave this money here," said

Ned. "And I don't want to be responsible for it."

Nancy suggested that they take it to police headquarters. "And I think I'll leave the key to the shop too."

"Good idea," Ned agreed. "Furthermore, I don't think you should come back here again without police protection."

The young sleuth nodded. She locked the door and the couple set off for police headquarters. Captain Turner was there. He took them into his private office and asked for the full story about Trunk Rasson.

After hearing it, he asked Nancy to make a formal complaint against the man so they could hold him. If it was true that Mr. Basswood had sent him to pick up certain objects, he had a legal right to do so.

"I'll confine my complaint to having been attacked," Nancy said.

When the formalities were over, she and Ned drove to the yacht club. The desk clerk said Mr. Ayer wanted to see Miss Lynbrook the minute she came in. Ned waited in the lobby while Nancy went to the manager's office.

"Hello," he said. "I have a message for you from George and it sounds important." His eyes twinkled.

"Don't keep me in suspense," Nancy said, smiling.

"The message was 'We trailed Basswood to the

Maple Motel in Pittville. He is registered there with Marco De Keer. Bess and Dick and I will wait for Nancy in the Robin Roost Restaurant until nine o'clock. It's located across the street.' "

"That really is news," Nancy told the manager. "Ned and I will go there at once. He showed up unexpectedly at the art shop and stayed to help me. By the way, we caught one of the men involved in the mystery."

"You did!" Mr. Ayer exclaimed. "Who is he?"

Nancy told him and asked if Mr. Ayer had ever heard of the trucker.

"No," he replied. "I guess his place of business isn't in Waterford."

Nancy said, "You're probably right, and added, "If George calls again, please tell her we're on our way." She and Ned set off at once.

It was an hour's drive to Pittville. They found the restaurant easily. Bess, George, and Dick had had an early dinner and they talked while Ned and Nancy ate.

"Mr. Basswood did not seem to suspect that he was being followed," Bess reported. "He went directly to Marco's barn and picked him up. Then they came here and are still in the motel."

Ned asked Dick how he liked being a detective.

"It's great," he replied. With a grin he added, "The first thing I found out was that Debbie Lynbrook is really Nancy Drew."

Bess blushed. "I'm sorry, Nancy, but I gave your secret away."

Nancy laughed. "The whole story may come out sooner than we thought." She and Ned briefed the others on their encounter with Trunk Rasson and what they had learned from him.

"You actually caught the intruder at the art shop?" Bess asked unbelievingly.

"We sure did," Ned told her. "I hope those iron muscles of his won't be able to break the bars of his jail cell!"

Nancy and Ned ate leisurely. Basswood and Marco De Keer did not appear.

On a hunch Nancy left the others to talk to the restaurant owner, Gus Becker. She asked him if he knew of anyone in town who might own a life-size marble statue of a woman.

"Yes, I do," he replied. "Mrs. Jonathan King. She has an estate on Tulip Road."

Nancy was thrilled by this bit of information and also at what followed. "Mrs. King is loaded with money," Gus went on. "She has a house full of paintings and statues, most of them from Italy."

"I believe I'll call on her," Nancy said. "Thank you very much."

When she returned to the table her friends could see excitement in her eyes. Ned asked, "You've picked up another clue?"

"A terrific one," Nancy replied, and told them

what Gus Becker had said. "It's only eight o'clock. Maybe we can see Mrs. King tonight. How about you going with me, Ned, while the rest of you watch for Mr. Basswood?"

They all agreed to the plan and Nancy went off to telephone Mrs. King.

CHAPTER XIX

Nancy in Marble

A MAN answered the telephone when Nancy dialed Mrs. King's home. After she had identified herself as Nancy Drew from River Heights, he said he would get Mrs. King.

"Hello," said a pleasant feminine voice. "This is Mrs. King. You are Miss Nancy Drew?"

"Yes, Mrs. King. Would it be possible for me and my friend Ned Nickerson to come and call on you? I understand you have a life-size marble statue of a young woman."

Nancy chuckled. "I'm trying to find one which I'm told looks like me. It's just possible yours is the right one."

Mrs. King laughed. "Yes, indeed, you may come. This is the most unusual reason anybody has ever given to see my statuary. Now I can't wait to meet you."

"We'll drive over right away."

Nancy returned to her friends and reported the phone conversation. "Come on, Ned. Let's go!"

She said they would return to the restaurant after their call on Mrs. King. "If you three trail Mr. Basswood, leave a note for us."

During the drive Nancy removed her wig and Ned heaved a sigh. "Now you look like your old self, and more my style."

Fifteen minutes later he was ringing the bell of the King mansion. It was a huge house at the end of a long uphill driveway.

A houseman opened the door. "Miss Drew and Mr. Nickerson?" he asked.

Ned said, "Yes."

"Please step in," the man requested. "I shall summon Mrs. King."

The house was exquisitely furnished with beautiful tapestry drapes, Oriental rugs, and fine furniture. On the walls of the rooms off the center hall were many valuable paintings. Graceful pieces of statuary on pedestals added to the artistic decor.

"What a gorgeous home!" Nancy murmured.

Ned nodded, then grinned. "Fit for a king!"

Nancy laughed at the pun, and turned toward the living room. Mrs. King rose from a chair and came into the hall. Her eyes opened wide upon seeing Nancy.

She held out both hands to the girl. "I'm delighted to meet you, Nancy. And I think your search has ended. You look exactly like my beautiful statue."

Then she turned to Ned. "Good evening," she said. "I'm so glad you both came. Well, I'm sure you're eager to see the statue so follow me."

Mrs. King led the way through the living room and a recreation room, then into a large glassed-in sunroom. It was decorated in pure white except for a few green palms and other plants attractively arranged around the room. The statue stood in the center of a plot of artificial grass.

Nancy and Ned gazed at it in awe. How fine and delicate it was!

Ned looked at Nancy, then at Mrs. King. He said, "Nancy could have posed for this."

"Indeed she could have," the woman agreed. "I've never heard that the statue had a name. I think now I'll call her Nancy."

The young sleuth smiled. "Does the statue whisper?"

Mrs. King looked surprised. "Whisper? No. Why did you ask?" She invited them to sit down.

Nancy told Mrs. King the story of the stolen whispering statue, including details of her search for it.

Ned interrupted. "Mrs. King, I think it only fair to tell you that Nancy is an amateur detective and has solved many cases. This is her latest."

Mrs. King sank back in her chair. "Stolen?" she repeated. "I had no idea!"

"I'm sorry to bring you such bad news," Nancy said. "The thief, or thieves, had a reproduction made which is very good but doesn't have the lovely patina this statue does."

"What are we going to do?" the woman asked. "As much as I love this piece, I don't want stolen property in my house. I'll cooperate with you in any way I can to find the culprit."

"Tell us," said Nancy, "who sold this statue to you?"

"An art dealer in New York City. He brought photos of the statue and I fell in love with it."

Mrs. King said the man was Thomas Mott. At Nancy's request she described him.

Ned spoke up. "He must be Mr. Atkin."

Nancy nodded and explained that Mr. Atkin was one of the men under suspicion.

Mrs. King said she had paid the art dealer five thousand dollars when he delivered the statue. "He came in a car followed by a truck."

"Did you see the man who was driving the truck?" Nancy queried.

"To tell the truth, I hardly noticed him. But he was a big man—and my, how strong! He carried the statue indoors by himself and it's very, very heavy.

"I have always felt," Mrs. King went on, "that I got the statue at a great bargain. I had it appraised since and was told it's worth much more than I paid for it."

Ned asked her if Mr. Mott had brought credentials.

"Oh yes," the woman replied. "He seemed very refined and showed me pictures of his shop in New York. I gave him a check, which he accepted without question."

"Well, I should think he would," Ned remarked, "and I'll bet he cashed it in a big hurry."

"Mrs. King," said Nancy, "by any chance do you still have your canceled check here? I'd like to see how it was endorsed."

Mrs. King stood up, saying she thought she could locate it easily. The woman went off. Nancy and Ned looked carefully at the statue to see if they could figure out what had made it whisper.

In a few minutes Mrs. King came back. "Here it is," she said, handing the check to Nancy.

The young sleuth turned it over. The Thomas Mott signature was in Mr. Basswood's handwriting!

"Mrs. King, this is another clue in the mystery," Nancy told her. "When a trial comes up, you may be asked to show the check."

"I'll be glad to," the gracious woman replied.

Nancy asked her if she would be willing to have a sculptor from New York City come and look at her statue. "He's Sylvester Holden, a friend of my father's."

"I've heard of Mr. Holden," said Mrs. King.

"May I use your phone to call him?" Nancy asked.

"Go ahead," said Mrs. King. "I'd be glad to have this thing settled. There's a phone in the recreation room."

Nancy went off to put in the call. Fortunately Mr. Holden was at home. He was astounded to learn what Nancy had found out and said he would be glad to come to Mrs. King's the day after tomorrow.

"Wonderful," said Nancy. "And please see if you can figure out why the statue used to whisper and doesn't any more."

Before going back to the other room, Nancy decided to telephone her father collect. He had just arrived home from Washington and was amazed to learn all that Nancy had been doing.

"My congratulations, dear. I think we should try to keep Atkin in the hospital. I know the superintendent. I'll explain why and ask him to talk to Atkin's doctor about keeping him there at least another day."

After saying good-by to her father, Nancy returned to the sunroom. She told Mrs. King that Mr. Holden would be there Friday.

"I hope to get back myself," Nancy added. "And now Ned and I must go. Friends of ours are waiting for us in town. And besides, we have to drive to the Waterford Yacht Club."

Mrs. King walked to the front door with her

guests and said again how delighted she was to have met them. She smiled. "I don't usually say that to people who bring me bad news."

Nancy and Ned chuckled and they both shook hands with her. Then they went outside and drove off. Nancy put on the long black wig and her sunglasses.

When the couple reached the restaurant, they found Bess, George, and Dick still there. The trio reported that Basswood and De Keer were still in the motel.

"We can't stay here all night," Bess spoke up. "What are we going to do about having the men watched?"

Nancy said she did not want to ask the police to do it. "After all, we need more evidence against the men. They could deny everything."

"That's right," Ned agreed. "How about a private detective agency? There must be one in town."

Nancy made the call and introduced herself as the daughter of Carson Drew. The agency knew him by reputation and said they would send a man over to talk to her. When he arrived the young people briefed him on the case.

He said, "If the men leave the motel, I'll follow them. Tomorrow morning I'll phone you, Miss Drew, about the result of my shadowing."

When Nancy and her friends were ready to leave, Ned said that as long as Nancy had a ride, he would go directly to the lake resort where he was staying. The others said good-by to him and climbed into Dick's sports car.

Upon reaching the yacht club, the girls thanked Dick for all his help. He grinned. "I wouldn't have missed it for anything."

While Nancy was getting ready for bed, her father telephoned. "I just had a call from the hospital superintendent," he reported. "Atkin sneaked out. Nobody knows where he went."

"Too bad," Nancy said. "I wonder if he knows where Mr. Basswood is."

"I imagine he plans to join him," Mr. Drew replied. "The police went to the house where Atkin boarded. He has not been there and left the hospital several hours ago."

Nancy suggested that perhaps Basswood and Marco De Keer were waiting for Atkin at the motel. When he arrived, they would take off.

"That's a good hunch," her father said. "If you hear anything, let me know."

In the morning the private detective called Nancy. He said that neither Basswood nor his companion had left the motel. Using Dick's car, she drove with Bess and George to police headquarters. The officers had no report on the owner of the art shop.

"May I have the key?" she requested. "I'd like to look around there again."

The sergeant on duty handed it over and said with a smile, "Keep in touch with us."

"I will," Nancy promised.

It was a gloomy day and the art shop was dark and rather chilly. The girls turned on all the lights. Everything was the same as Nancy had left it the day before.

Bess hunched her shoulders. "Ugh, it's dismal and spooky in here! Let's go!"

Before Nancy could answer, a customer knocked on the front door.

Bess begged her not to open the door, but Nancy said, "I may as well wait on the person."

Within five minutes two other customers arrived and the three girls found themselves having a busy morning. By noontime they had taken in a sizable sum of money.

George remarked, "Basswood certainly isn't going to pay you any salary. Why don't you just quit the job? I'm sure you aren't going to find any more clues here."

Nancy was inclined to agree and finally said she would lock the place.

"Thank goodness," said Bess. "My feet hurt from being on them all morning. Let's go to that sandwich shop where we can sit down and get something to eat."

"First we'll go to the police," George told her. "We aren't going to carry all this money around."

They walked to headquarters. Nancy turned in the cash and the key and said that she was locking the shop for the day. She suggested that the officers keep an eye on it.

"We'll do that," the sergeant told her.

While the girls were eating, Nancy said she wanted to drive to De Keer's barn studio. "To see if he too has moved out."

Before heading for the barn, Nancy telephoned Ned to ask if he would like to go along. He agreed, saying he would meet her there as soon as he could.

When they reached the barn, the girls found it wide open and apparently nothing had been taken from either the inside or the outside. But De Keer was not there. A tall, heavy-set man was busy brushing a rubbery material over a statue to make a mold.

Nancy asked when Mr. De Keer would arrive. The answer startled her. "He won't be back," the man said. "My name is Herbert Michaels and I'm the new owner. What do you want?"

"I'm looking for an inexpensive statuette," Nancy replied.

"Well, look around," Mr. Michaels said. "I can't leave this job right now."

The girls sensed that the man was watching them closely so they separated to look around the place. Nancy became intrigued with the two hollowed-out halves of a life-size reproduction. It lay on the floor near the rear door of the barn.

"I'd like to ask Mr. Michaels about it," Nancy thought, but at the moment he and her friends were out of sight.

As Nancy examined the reproduction, two huge arms encircled her shoulders. She started to scream, but a gag was jammed into her mouth. Her efforts to free herself were futile. The next moment Nancy was pushed into one half of the statue and the other half was fastened into place on top of her.

Within seconds the statue was lifted, carried a distance, and laid down. As Nancy became drowsy from the lack of enough air, she heard a motor start. She was in some kind of vehicle, being driven away!

CHAPTER XX

A Startling Revelation

THOUGH Nancy had panicked when she was encased in the statue, she finally managed to overcome her fright. Her first thought was, "I can breathe. There must be holes in this statue, and they're near my head."

The vehicle was traveling at a fast speed and the statue jounced badly.

"I wonder how long my kidnapper will keep me in here," she asked herself. Then a horrifying thought came to her. "Maybe he doesn't intend to let me out. He may drop me off some place and leave me to starve to death! Oh, Ned, why didn't you come?"

Back at the barn Bess and George were searching for Nancy. When they did not find her and discovered that Mr. Michaels was gone, they began calling Nancy's name. There was no answer and they were concerned.

"Look!" Bess exclaimed. "The two halves of that life-size statue are gone." She grabbed her cousin's arm. "Do you suppose Nancy could have been put in it and carried off in a car?"

George was stunned by the thought but admitted that Bess was probably right. She rushed to the rear door. "The truck is gone!" she cried out.

The girls rushed around the barn looking for a clue as to where Nancy might have been taken.

"Here's her wig!" Bess called. "It's not far from where the two halves of that statue lay on the floor."

At that moment a car pulled into the driveway. George and Bess went to the door to see who was arriving.

Ned and Dick!

"Oh boys!" Bess yelled. "Nancy has been kidnapped!"

"What!" Ned and Dick burst out. "When? How did it happen?"

The girls told their story and Dick said, "Ned was afraid there might be trouble here. So he picked me up and we rushed over. And now we're too late!"

"Maybe not," said Ned. "We can try to follow the tire treads of the man's truck on the macadam road. By the way, who was he?"

"He gave his name as Michaels," George replied as she hurried to Ned's car.

Bess paused to pick up Nancy's purse and her

wig. Evidently the young sleuth had struggled with her abductor and the wig had come off. Bess got into Dick's car and they followed Ned.

There was little conversation between Ned and George, but both were thinking, "We must overtake that truck. I hope we'll be in time to save Nancy!"

Both Ned and Dick were driving as fast as they dared and fifteen minutes later they saw a truck in the distance.

"Is that the one?" Ned asked George.

As he drew closer, she said excitedly, "Yes! Yes, it is!"

The two boys put on a burst of speed and came alongside the truck. Gradually they edged it toward the side of the road, hoping to make the driver stop. But he was determined not to and yelled at Ned to get out of the way.

"Here comes a state trooper!" George cried out.

Ned waved his arm out the window signaling for the trooper to stop the truck. The officer in turn waved the driver over and in a moment Michaels was forced to come to a halt.

At once he opened the cab door and tried to flee. But the trooper and Dick grabbed him.

"You got no right to stop me!" the prisoner growled. "Take your hands off me!"

"As soon as we find out what you're carrying in the back of your truck," Dick told him.

Ned, Bess, and George by now had opened the rear doors of the truck and climbed inside. The statue lay on the floor.

"Nancy! Nancy!" Ned cried as he tried to find a way to break the statue open.

Bess was crying. George was biting her lips to keep tears back. Would they find their best friend still alive?

Ned had pulled out a sharp penknife and was gouging a hole into the top of the terra-cotta figure. Finally he accomplished it.

"Nancy!" he called inside. To his relief there was a mumbled response.

By this time the trooper and Dick had brought their prisoner to the rear of the truck.

"Break this open!" Ned ordered Michaels.

With no choice but to obey, Michaels jumped inside. From a back pocket he took out a small chisel and hammer. Within a few minutes Nancy's head was exposed. Ned yanked the gag from her mouth.

"I'm—I'm okay," she murmured.

Michaels finally pried the entire statue apart. Nancy was released. After several gulps of fresh air she was able to stand up by herself. She looked bitterly at her kidnapper but was too weak to say anything.

"I didn't mean any harm," Michaels shouted. "This wasn't my idea."

"Whose was it?" the trooper asked.

"They'll kill me if I tell you," the man answered.

In a hoarse voice Nancy whispered, "Trunk Rasson."

Ned added, "Officer, Trunk's in jail. He probably expected Michaels to come and bail him out but he didn't do it."

Michaels' bravado suddenly vanished. "Okay," he said. "But we're only two of the gang. I'm not going to tell you who the rest are. Right now the safest place for me would probably be jail."

The trooper asked if either of the boys knew how to drive the truck. Dick said that he sometimes used the one that belonged to the yacht club.

"Then will you drive this truck to police headquarters? Ned, you join him in the cab."

As he spoke, the trooper took handcuffs from his pocket and fastened Michaels' hands together behind his back. The motorcycle was lifted into the truck and the trooper and his prisoner climbed in. Nancy drove Ned's car and George took the wheel of Dick's.

A little later they arrived at headquarters and charges were preferred against Michaels. He was led off to a cell.

"What about Basswood and De Keer?" Ned asked Nancy.

She offered to telephone the motel and see if

the suspects were still there. Nancy learned that they were in their room. She wondered if they were waiting for one or both of their confederates who were now prisoners.

The young sleuth then telephoned her father. He was astounded and relieved at her news.

"I'll take over now," he said, "and call Mrs. King. I'd like to arrange for all of us to be at her house tomorrow morning at ten o'clock, and Mr. Holden will be there too. I'll ask Mrs. Merriam to drive out also."

When the young people arrived at the King mansion the following day, they were astonished to find Basswood, Atkin, and De Keer there and three policemen. Mr. Drew listed the evidence that his daughter and her friends had amassed against the thieves. "That—together with Mrs. King's positive identification of Atkin as the man who delivered the statue—is more than enough reason for holding these men."

The prisoners sullenly refused to answer questions. But when Basswood recognized Nancy, he cried out, "Your hair! You were wearing a wig that half-covered your face! You're Nancy Drew, not Debbie Lynbrook!"

Mrs. King had extra chairs brought to her living room. Everyone sat down, then Mr. Drew addressed the group.

"First of all, I want our prisoners to know that Trunk Rasson and Michaels who followed George and Bess and me one night in River Heights have confessed everything they did. Other parts of the operation have been learned through some skillful sleuthing."

He did not mention Nancy by name but gave her a broad smile. He said that Basswood, under the alias of Thomas Mott, had a sizable bank account in New York City. Certain deposits were payments received from the sale of the stolen whispering statue and from Mrs. Merriam's books. The woman had been paid only a small percentage of the money Basswood had received.

Bess was furious to hear this. She whispered to George, "How crooked can a person be!"

Mr. Drew further revealed that De Keer had made numerous reproductions which had been sold as originals, with Basswood finding purchasers. "They were always sold to uninformed but wealthy persons. According to Trunk Rasson, Basswood used many aliases and several strong-arm men. The three at the deserted mansion on the Waterford beach were among them. Basswood had sent the fake movers to steal the reproduction from the yacht club to avoid its being detected as a copy."

The art dealer jumped up from his chair and shouted, "It's not true! I'm innocent! I'll fight this!"

Atkin, who had been silent up to this time,

exclaimed, "It's no use, Basswood! We may as well give up. It'll go easier for us."

Basswood hissed at his assistant, "Shut up!"

Mr. Drew ordered him to be quiet. "You can do your arguing in court. Right now, I want everyone to transfer to the room where the whispering statue is."

This announcement unnerved Atkin completely. He slumped in his chair and everyone thought he was going to have another heart attack. But he finally got up and strode with the others to the sunroom. Mr. Holden stood near the marble lady and began to talk.

"This used to be known as the whispering statue. After it was stolen, Marco De Keer made a mold of it so he could cast a reproduction. He ruined the whispering quality. It was through a clue I got from Nancy Drew that I have been able to restore it."

There were gasps from his audience. Mr. Holden smiled. "I'd like Nancy to tell you herself how she guessed this."

As the young sleuth hesitated, half a dozen people said, "Speech! Speech! Come on, Nancy!"

She walked slowly to Mr. Holden's side, then said, "When I was a prisoner inside the unfinished statue, I noticed that two holes had been put in it so I could breathe. I suspect De Keer and Basswood knew I'd be coming back to the barn to hunt for more clues, and had the two halves of the statue all ready, hoping to capture me."

Dick looked puzzled. "But I thought they didn't know that you were Nancy Drew," he said.

"I didn't," Basswood said. "But even Debbie Lynbrook got to know too much and she had to be held for a while until all of us could clear out."

George asked, "If you suspected her, why did you let her have the key to your shop?"

The art dealer answered, "She was an excellent saleswoman and I figured she could sell everything in the place before I skipped out. But my plans went wrong. She caught Rasson, who was supposed to bring all the money she made to me."

Mr. Holden interrupted. "Shall we proceed with the explanation about the whispering statue?"

There was a chorus of yeses from the audience.

Nancy went on, "As air came through the holes in the statue in which I was a prisoner it made weird little sounds. This gave me the idea that perhaps the original statue had had some concealed holes in it which caused the whispering sounds. When Mr. De Keer painted the rubbery material over it to make his mold, he covered them up. This was fortunate for him because now the statue could not be traced so easily by the police."

"She's right," Mr. Holden declared. "I've

found the holes which had been cleverly put in originally. There was one inside each ear and two under locks of hair at the nape of the neck."

"Have you opened them?" Bess asked eagerly.

"Yes, this morning. We will now move the statue outdoors. The wind is blowing strongly in the garden."

Mrs. King summoned her houseman who brought a dolly and the marble lady was trundled into the garden and set up. Everyone gathered around it.

The statue was indeed whispering and Bess declared it was saying "Woe to anyone who doesn't speak the truth!"

Suddenly Basswood cried out, "I can't stand it! That thing's supernatural! I'll tell the truth!"

His confession was mostly a reiteration of what Nancy and her friends and Mr. Drew had found out, but he did promise to return every penny of the money he had acquired dishonestly.

Nancy had guessed correctly that De Keer had made the reproduction to cover up the theft of the original statue. He had brought it to the yacht club and almost been caught, so he had put it in the abandoned tool shed. There had never been another chance for him to set it in place.

Basswood faced De Keer. "If you hadn't put your initials on the bottom of that reproduction, we'd never have been found out!" he accused his friend.

Mr. Drew interrupted him. "There was plenty of other evidence against you," he said.

Basswood went on, "De Keer made several stupid mistakes. He should never have made that threatening telephone call to your home, Mr. Drew. And he shouldn't have sent Rasson and his buddy to your house. Those two things put you on our trail right away. Another thing. He shouldn't have gone to the yacht club at night to punch those holes in his reproduction after your daughter stopped my other men from taking it."

De Keer shot back, "Basswood, you messed matters up yourself by having that blank telegram delivered and having the masked man try to sink the sailboat Nancy and her friend George were in! But the worst thing you did was to hire her as a salesclerk! Nancy Drew right under your nose!"

The police officers said it was time for them to take their prisoners away. The confessions had been recorded on tape.

After the group had gone, Nancy and her father and all their friends continued to gaze at the beautiful marble statue.

As the young detective stood there, she wondered what challenge lay ahead. Where would it lead her? This question was answered very soon. At that moment events were taking place that would involve her in the amazing mystery of *The Haunted Bridge*.

Interrupting Nancy's thoughts, Mrs. King said

that if the members of the yacht club were willing, she would like to keep the statue. When she received a reimbursement from Basswood, she would turn the five thousand dollars and some extra money over to the club.

Mrs. Merriam spoke up. "That's very generous of you. And Mr. Drew and Nancy, I never can thank you enough for all you've done for me."

There was a slight pause, then Mrs. King said, "Listen! I believe the statue is whispering something to our young sleuth."

As everyone became quiet, there was a strong gust of wind.

Mr. Holden smiled. "Did you hear that? I think the statue is saying 'Thank you, Nancy Drew, for giving me back my voice.' "

ORDER FORM

NANCY DREW
MYSTERY STORIES®

by Carolyn Keene

Now that you've met Nancy Drew. we're sure you'll want to read the thrilling adventures in the *Nancy Drew Mystery Stories®*

To make it easy for you to own all the books in this action-packed series, we've enclosed this handy order form.

58 TITLES AT YOUR BOOKSELLER OR
COMPLETE THIS HANDY COUPON AND MAIL TO:

GROSSET & DUNLAP, INC.
P.O. Box 941, Madison Square Post Office, New York, N.Y. 10010

Please send me the *Nancy Drew®* books checked below. My check or money order for $_____ is enclosed and includes 50¢ *per book* postage and handling. (Please *do not* send cash.)

The Nancy Drew Mystery Stories® @ $3.95 each:

☐	1.	Secret of the Old Clock	9501-7	☐	29.	Mystery at the Ski Jump	9529-7
☐	2.	Hidden Staircase	9502-5	☐	30.	Clue of the Velvet Mask	9530-0
☐	3.	Bungalow Mystery	9503-3	☐	31.	Ringmaster's Secret	9531-9
☐	4.	Mystery at Lilac Inn	9504-1	☐	32.	Scarlet Slipper Mystery	9532-7
☐	5.	Secret of Shadow Ranch	9505-X	☐	33.	Witch Tree Symbol	9533-5
☐	6.	Secret of Red Gate Farm	9506-8	☐	34.	Hidden Window Mystery	9534-3
☐	7.	Clue in the Diary	9507-6	☐	35.	Haunted Showboat	9535-1
☐	8.	Nancy's Mysterious Letter	9508-4	☐	36.	Secret of the Golden Pavilion	9536-X
☐	9.	The Sign of the Twisted Candles	9509-2	☐	37.	Clue in the Old Stagecoach	9537-8
☐	10.	Password to Larkspur Lane	9510-6	☐	38.	Mystery of the Fire Dragon	9538-6
☐	11.	Clue of the Broken Locket	9511-4	☐	39.	Clue of the Dancing Puppet	9539-4
☐	12.	The Message in the Hollow Oak	9512-2	☐	40.	Moonstone Castle Mystery	9540-8
☐	13.	Mystery of the Ivory Charm	9513-0	☐	41.	Clue of the Whistling Bagpipes	9541-6
☐	14.	The Whispering Statue	9514-9	☐	42.	Phantom of Pine Hill	9542-4
☐	15.	Haunted Bridge	9515-7	☐	43.	Mystery of the 99 Steps	9543-2
☐	16.	Clue of the Tapping Heels	9516-5	☐	44.	Clue in the Crossword Cipher	9544-0
☐	17.	Mystery of the Brass Bound Trunk	9517-3	☐	45.	Spider Sapphire Mystery	9545-9
☐	18.	Mystery at Moss-Covered Mansion	9518-1	☐	46.	The Invisible Intruder	9546-7
				☐	47.	The Mysterious Mannequin	9547-5
☐	19.	Quest of the Missing Map	9519-X	☐	48.	The Crooked Banister	9548-3
☐	20.	Clue in the Jewel Box	9520-3	☐	49.	The Secret of Mirror Bay	9549-1
☐	21.	The Secret in the Old Attic	9521-1	☐	50.	The Double Jinx Mystery	9550-5
☐	22.	Clue in the Crumbling Wall	9522-X	☐	51.	Mystery of the Glowing Eye	9551-3
☐	23.	Mystery of the Tolling Bell	9523-8	☐	52.	The Secret of the Forgotten City	9552-1
☐	24.	Clue in the Old Album	9524-6	☐	53.	The Sky Phantom	9553-X
☐	25.	Ghost of Blackwood Hall	9525-4	☐	54.	The Strange Message In the Parchment	9554-8
☐	26.	Clue of the Leaning Chimney	9526-2				
☐	27.	Secret of the Wooden Lady	9527-0	☐	55.	Mystery of Crocodile Island	9555-6
☐	28.	The Clue of the Black Keys	9528-9	☐	56.	The Thirteenth Pearl	9556-4

SHIP TO:

NAME _____
(please print)

ADDRESS _____

CITY _____ STATE _____ ZIP _____